MURDER IS SKIN DEEP

M.G. COLE

TANGLEBOX
BOOKS

MURDER
IS SKIN DEEP

MURDER IS SKIN DEEP
A DCI Garrick mystery - Book 2

Copyright © 2021 by Max Cole (M.G.Cole)

Cover art: Shutterstock

1

Anybody can commit a murder. Getting away with it, that's what takes real skill.

The crunch of broken glass underfoot would wake nobody this morning. A chill breeze through the broken double-glazed patio doors brought with it a smattering of rain that cast dark spots across the parchment-coloured Saxony carpet. Manoeuvring the body in the living room was more difficult than expected, especially when the limp foot caught on the leg of the coffee table and dragged it along, spilling several luxury lifestyle magazines to the floor.

The body was positioned in front of the eighty-five-inch Samsung television. A quick search for the remote control, and the television came to life with a dreary reality show in which a gormless bunch of talentless nobodies complained about their privileged lifestyles. The volume inched upwards until one girl's shrill regional accent became a banshee wail. It was an appropriate harbinger of death. A moment was needed to make sure everything was in place.

This is how it should be. Unhurried. Careful. This way, mistakes are not made.

The faint rise and fall of the prone man's snug-fitting Hugo Boss shirt verified he was still breathing.

Just.

That was something else a murder required: a victim.

The gun felt almost like a toy; old and uncared for. Only its weight hinted at its lethal potential. The loud reports were almost deafening in the enclosed room. But the shots were on target, creating a pair of deep-red roses across the shirt, and causing the body to jerk as it absorbed the impact. It was almost hypnotic to watch the stains grow to fist size blotches. Then blood seeped from beneath the victim as it poured from the exit wound and oozed across the carpet.

The execution was complete.

There was little point in hanging around. The catch on the victim's Rolex only came free on the third attempt, and it was removed from the swollen limp wrist. A quick riffle through the wallet on the dining room table confirmed there was no cash inside. Now it was time to leave.

They say murder is easy.

This one would look like it was.

"And you've heard nothing for the last few weeks?"

The top of Dr Amy Harman's pen swayed to-and-fro over her pad in an almost hypnotic motion. Her blue eyes narrowed behind the red-framed glasses as she sized DCI David Garrick up.

Garrick pulled his gaze away and fixed it on a potted plant sitting on the window ledge. The soil was dry, and the edges of the leaves were slightly crinkled and turning brown. He hoped the good doctor looked after her patients' mental health better than she did the office flora.

"It was just that one time. I've received tons of blank calls, but they hang up a couple of seconds after the answerphone kicks in. Typical cold callers," he assured her.

It had been several weeks since he received a phone call he had sworn was from his sister. His sister who was murdered on the other side of the Atlantic months earlier. At the time he'd been under a considerable amount of pressure from a case he was leading, and a recent health diagnosis had compounded his worries.

After taking compassionate leave over his sister's death, Dr Harman had been assigned to him as a condition for his return to work. She was an angel and a curse. He didn't have anybody to talk to about his inner turmoil. No family. No friends, well, not anymore. Having an attractive woman hang on his every word was a novelty for Garrick, even if she was being paid for it and analysing every syllable to gauge his mental health.

Which is why he had regretted telling her about answering a call from his dead sister. His damage limitation strategy hadn't been a great idea either. He had hurriedly placed the blame on the growth that had been found pressing on his brain. It must have been a side effect of the medication or a manifestation of his worry. He couldn't stop himself from throwing half-arsed solutions at her. If he went on much longer, he would probably give her all the ammunition she needed to eject him off the force.

Harman assured him she was there solely to assess his mental wellbeing; his physical was somebody else's problem. She'd been more than understanding and, prior to their next session, had taken the time to research similar cases. Coupled with the fact that the very evening of the alleged phone call, he had been warned by his consultant to avoid any head trauma, Garrick had an entire bookcase fall on him and had lain unconscious from smoke inhalation. She assured him that would have been enough for *anybody* to hear voices.

Garrick had downplayed the incident, but it had really shaken him. He'd even telephoned the police department in Flora, Illinois, to check if there had any further developments in the case. There had been none.

The focus of Garrick's stress had then shifted to the

mischievous growth in his head. A biopsy would tell if it was malignant or not, but that that procedure had been postponed when his consultant had sought a second opinion and decided they should monitor its growth. Two MRI scans later, and the news was that it hadn't grown at all.

"Schrodinger's cat," Dr Harman said, picking up his train of thought.

"Mmm?"

"It's a quantum physics thought experiment about a cat in a box. The cat's being potentially poisoned, but you can only truly tell if it's alive or dead by opening the box."

Garrick shifted position in the chair. He'd been there so long it felt as if it was moulding to his shape.

"You'd hear it scratching."

"That's not the point. It's a soundproof box. You can't hear or see the cat."

"Murders I can handle," he said with a wry smile. "But hurt a cat, and it will take more than the law to save you."

Harman gave a good-natured chuckle. Or was she humouring him?

"How people treat animals reveals a lot about them." Garrick waited to hear if that was a good thing or not, but she tapped the tip of the pen gently against her lips and looked thoughtful. "What I meant with Schrodinger's cat is, not wanting to know the truth is actually a prevalent attitude with most people. For example, not knowing how much debt you're in means the debt can't be so bad. Not knowing your fiancé is cheating on you, means life continues as normal."

Garrick glanced at her. That was an unusual analogy to throw at him. Had it been a slip of the tongue? Dr Harman was looking at her plant, as if noticing the withering leaves for the first time. Her shoulder length wavy blonde hair was tied back today. Garrick hated himself for noticing. He hated finding her attractive. Flirting with one's therapist was surely a textbook act of insanity.

"I'm still not sure why you brought the cat into this."

She smiled and looked squarely at him. "The biopsy. You still don't have a date for it, correct?" Garrick nodded. "Which could be something of a relief, because right now you're in a state of not knowing. Ignorance is bliss."

"Not in my profession."

"No. But in life it's a self-defence mechanism that keeps stress at bay. It allows you to focus on more pressing matters in hand. And that can be a good thing, as long as you don't let ignorance become your reality."

Garrick let that sink in for a moment. Harman loved oblique associations, cryptic analogies, and tenuous allegories. "Are you fishing around about what happened with John?"

John Howard had been a long-time friend. And, unbeknownst to him, a serial killer on the side. A difficult proposition to accept about the closest friend he had.

"Well, *you* mentioned him, not me."

Garrick raised an eyebrow. "Dr Harman, if we were in court then you would be accused of leading the witness."

"Is that what *you* think?"

"Now you're venturing down the lane of quackery," Garrick laughed. "I respect you too much for that."

He caught a flash of a smile as she noted something on the pad.

"You're too sharp for me, Detective." She glanced at her Apple Watch. "And we're almost out of time, which means you avoided the questions I was going to ask about whether your date made it to the next round."

He had managed two more rounds with Wendy after their disastrous first date. Incredibly, she had reached out to him after that, and the next two dates had gone well. Slow, but well. But he didn't want to let Dr Harman know that. Not yet.

"Too bad," Garrick replied as he stood. "At least we have a subject for the next session."

Dr Harman sharply tapped the pen on her pad.

"It's so much easier when *you* set the agenda."

Garrick smiled, but couldn't help thinking that she had just set him up. On the way to his aging beige Land Rover, he pulled the collar of his Barbour tight against the rain and tried to remember whose turn was it to set the date. He was pretty sure it was Wendy's.

He checked his phone to see if she had messaged him as it had been on silent during his session. There were three missed calls and a voicemail from DS Okon. That could mean only one thing.

3

It was still raining heavily when Garrick pulled up outside the driveway of the detached house in Tenterden. He didn't need to check the address. The police car at the entrance gate was enough to confirm this was the murder scene. He showed his ID card to the copper, who told him to park further up the street.

It was difficult to find a parking spot on the narrow road, and by the time Garrick jogged back to the house and up the gravel driveway, his pants were soaked through.

The house was an impressive size and had been heavily renovated from its Georgian origins. Even from just the lights from the police vans, he could see the front garden was fastidiously maintained. The twenty yards of gravel driveway were taken up by two marked incident vans and a police car. The forensic team was putting up a tent against an extended wing of the house. The front door was open, with a policewoman standing just inside. When he showed his ID, he was directed into a large living room, filled with more white suited forensics being watched by a young Nigerian detective, DS Chibarameze Okon.

"Hi Chib, what have we got?"

Chib frowned when she noticed Garrick's coat was dripping on the plastic that had been laid to protect the floor. Somehow, it looked as if the rain had missed her completely. Taking the hint, Garrick removed his jacket and shoes, placing them on the plastic. Chib tossed him a rolled-up pair of blue plastic over-shoes, which he dutifully placed over his socks. He noticed she was wearing hers over her sensible flat shoes. He took a pair of blue latex gloves from his pocket and put them on.

"Owner of the house." She nodded to the body on the floor. "Derek Fraser."

He was sprawled out in front of the television, with two large pools of dried blood extending from his shoulders and back like macabre angel wings. A large brickwork fireplace stood next to the TV and blackened logs and fragments of burnt papers showed it was still in use. The rest of the furnishings were all sleek and modern. A pale brown leather sofa, the end of which curved to sit five people, dominated the wall opposite the television. A large silver reading lamp hung over the corner. The metallic domed lampshade looked more at home in a science fiction film. The coffee table was handcrafted and modern, with multiple issues of magazines on it: Luxury Life, Country Life, Kent Life, Boat Owner, Flying Magazine, and Conde Nast Traveller.

The television was huge and kitted out with a Sky Q box and a surround sound bar. A pair of paintings hung on the wall. Garrick was no art connoisseur, and these looked amateurish, so he assumed they were collectibles. The sort coveted by people with no taste and lots of money.

Across the room was a solid oak dining table large enough to seat ten, with uncomfortable-looking narrow backed chairs neatly tucked all around. Beyond that was an open double-doorway into a kitchen that looked expensively appointed. At the opposite end of the living room an extension had been added, looking onto the front garden where Garrick had arrived. The glass from one of the smashed patio doors littered the floor with thousands of fragments.

"Burglary?" said Garrick as they moved closer to the body. Derek Fraser wore red trousers, a white shirt, and still had a pair of tan loafers on.

Chib read through the notes on her pad, all written in precise, neat script. "Maybe. Derek Frasier, 52, divorcee." Frasier's hair was a lush premature white, and his skin looked tanned as if from a recent holiday. Beyond that, his face was a mess of swelling and contusions. "Looks like somebody beat the heck out of him before shooting him." Two broken teeth showed behind his death rictus.

"That looks like frenzied work." Garrick glanced around but couldn't see any photographs of the man himself. He wondered if the victim's own mother would struggle to ID him. The blood had dried and solidified on the carpet fibres. "He's been here for a fair bit."

"Over twenty-four hours, they reckon," Chib glanced at the forensic team.

"Who found him?"

"An Amazon delivery driver." She indicated to a small package on the dining table. "Said he rang the bell before he noticed the patio was smashed open. The TV was on really loud. That's what drew his attention. He came in through there," Chib indicated to the broken door. "Found him dead. He muted the TV and rang 999."

"SOCO found anything useful yet?"

Chib shook her head. "*Forensics* say it looks like the glass was broken with a hammer. We don't know yet. Then it was used to bludgeon him to near-death. Then our killer shot him twice for good measure."

Garrick knelt to get a closer look at the body. The left shirt sleeve was inched up, revealing deep indentations of watch strap. "Maybe his watch was stolen."

Chib moved to the table and gestured to an open wallet. "This was left. No cash inside, but the credit cards are still there."

"Maybe our killer took whatever cash there was and left the plastic. That's pretty common, as it makes little sense to be caught using a dead man's credit card."

"But why leave the TV?"

"That's a two-man job to get it out of here. Nothing looks ransacked. It's not as if he was searching for anything in particular. He wouldn't hang around after killing him. He takes what he can and legs it." Even as he spoke the words, Garrick felt there was something missing.

"There's no sign of a struggle."

"Mmm. What about a phone? Computer? Tablet?"

"Nothing yet, but we haven't searched the kitchen or upstairs." Chib crossed to the patio, careful not to disturb the broken glass. "So, our burglar breaks in here. Maybe Fraser heard nothing because of the TV's volume. He crosses to here," she took ten steps to the coffee table. "They have an altercation. Mr Fraser gets struck in the face with whatever the thief used to break the glass and is killed." She cocked the fingers of the right hand to imitate a gun. "Then he's shot twice for good measure." She gingerly stepped around the bloodstains on the carpet. "Our killer dashes to the table where he sees the wallet. Takes what he can. Then, worried that the gunshots may have alerted somebody, he makes his way out the same way he got in."

Garrick stood up and scratched the bristles of two days' worth of growth as he looked around the room, picturing the moves Chib had suggested.

"If the intruder came with a gun, that sounds premeditated. If it was Fraser's, then it sounds like an act of desperation." He crossed to the Amazon package on the table. It was still taped closed. He left it for forensics to open. "Okay. The driver said the TV was on loud? How loud?" He spotted the TV remote on the floor, under the coffee table. He retrieved it and thumbed the standby button. The Samsung came to life with a raucous US crime show. It was so loud that the forensic team all jolted in surprise.

Garrick pointed at the TV and spoke to Chib, but his words were lost. She shook her head and yelled back but was barely audible.

"What did you say?"

Garrick stabbed the power button, killing the TV. "How could he hear the glass being broken when the intruder came in?"

"Maybe he was in the room or the kitchen? And just saw him?"

Garrick moved into the kitchen. It was dark, but after two attempts at finding the light switches, he turned them on. As he had glimpsed, it was a beautifully laid out kitchen with a central island, over which a rack of copper pans hung. A granite worktop ran around the edge. A large American-style fridge-freezer stood in the corner. An impressive gas-range cooker ran along one wall. The oven and microwave were discreetly blended amongst the cupboards. There was another patio door that looked across the dark rear garden. Garrick ran his fingers over the granite work surface, then looked back into the living room. It offered a partial line of sight to the extension.

"If the time of death was after five, he would have probably had the lights on rather than stand here in the dark." It was March, and the daylight hours still felt far too short. "And it doesn't look like the thief searched in here either, unless we're dealing with a particularly tidy criminal."

He moved back into the living room and frowned. "And if Fraser was in here, then he would have seen the bloke break the window. Double glazing is tough. It doesn't always break first time. He should've had enough time to dial 999."

"Assuming he had a mobile. I can't see a landline." Chib frowned. "Then he must have been elsewhere in the house and walked in on him." Garrick nodded. "But there were no other lights on. Not in the hall or upstairs." She pointed to the door Garrick had entered through. "There's another reception room through there with a pool table and a running machine. The lights were off."

"He could have turned them off as he was passing through, before seeing the intruder. And if the TV was on loud, he may have been trying to listen to it from another room."

"If the killer was already inside as Fraser entered, then he would have caught him by surprise because the TV would have drowned out any warnings he may have shouted. Our intruder would have turned," Chib mimed the movements of the killer, raising her hand as if wielding a hammer, "and struck him in the face." She smiled, satisfied with her reasoning. "They struggled." She moved around the room, closer to the body. "And he fell here. Then he was shot."

Garrick chewed his lip thoughtfully.

"Why break the window?"

"How else was he going to get in?"

"I know it's a quiet area, and the driveway is a way back from the road, even so, wouldn't the back garden be a more secluded point of entry than the front? And if it was the only room in the house lit up, then our burglar would know there was somebody in, especially if he could hear the TV. So why break-in here?"

Chib opened her mouth to answer but couldn't think of anything logical to say. She shrugged.

"What about his car?"

"There's a Mercedes S-Class Coupé in the garage. But as you said, a petty crook wouldn't take that, would he?"

Garrick circled his finger around the room. "This isn't gelling for me. It feels more deliberate."

"Like a hit?"

Garrick met her gaze and raised his eyebrows as if to say, *why not*? He turned to the victim on the floor. "We need to find out everything about our Mr Fraser. Who is he exactly?"

4

K ent's Serious Crimes Department was in a poky austere building in Maidstone, a hangover from hasty post-war rebuilding. It was a far cry from the spacious old Sutton Road HQ, which was sold off due to budget cuts. With a seemingly constant chill blowing through ill-fitting windows and suffering from intermittent heating, it wasn't the most pleasant place to work. Although Garrick's team were universally relieved not to have been moved to Northfleet, they feared it was just a matter of time.

The overnight rain had swelled the banks of the River Medway as it churned a brown soup through the city, but the sun had come out this morning, bringing with it the first real hint of spring. A new start. But not for Derek Fraser.

DC Fanta Liu pinned a photograph of the victim on the evidence wall. She stood on tiptoes as far as her petite five-five frame would allow, provoking sniggers from DC Harry Lord, who was a couple of years older than Garrick. A sharp look from DC Sean Wilkes silenced him. Fanta ignored the heckles. After their last major incident, she was riding high after being congratulated on her input and was feeling bulletproof. She addressed the team.

"Our deceased is Derek Alan Fraser. 46, killed in his home in Tenterden." The photograph showed a strikingly handsome man with his arm around a woman, both against the backdrop of an azure sea. Even with a mane of thick white hair, he looked young. "This piccy is fourteen months old, sent by his ex-wife. Rebecca Ellis. She uses her maiden name and is living in Portugal. She didn't sound to cut up when I spoke to her. She claimed they had an acrimonious divorce and seemed quite proud that she'd taken him to the cleaners."

Garrick harrumphed. "Judging by his car and house, he was doing pretty well anyway. What did he do?"

Chib spoke up, sitting on the edge of her desk as Fanta placed pins in a map of the area. "He was an art dealer. Mostly working with a gallery in Rye." Fanta dutifully placed a pin in the small East Sussex coastal town. "But before that he had a chequered history." She read from a printout. "He ran a scrapyard outside Tunbridge Wells and was nicked for fencing stolen cars, which he sold at a small dealership he had in Tonbridge. He did two years for that. After that, he was implicated in a marketing scam, extracting money from pensioners for new boiler systems that either never arrived or were installed so poorly that Harry here would look an expert."

Harry Lord held up his hands as if to say, *what did I do?*

"I'm starting to dislike our poor deceased wretch," said Garrick. He hated the moment in a case when he had to immerse himself into the victim's life. It often brought up unfulfilled dreams and hopes that had been cancelled by an act of barbarity. Such details turned a lifeless corpse into a fully rounded human being. It was the worst part of the job. Having a victim that he actively disliked would improve matters no end.

"He wasn't formally convicted of anything in that instance, but his company folded. We're still looking into his work history, but it seems he started making an honest mark in the art world with some new up-and-comer. An artist only known as Hoy. The first few had only sold for a couple of hundred quid, but the last one reached thirty grand. It gained Fraser a bit of fame. He recently had a feature in Country Life magazine and Kent Life. We have digital copies on the article on HOLMES."

"Clocking up an honest reputation?" Garrick pulled a face. "Cause of death?"

"Two gunshots to the chest."

Fanta put up a picture of the corpse. This time the SOCOs had placed small plastic number tags on the wound and at various points on the carpet. Then she pinned up a photograph of Fraser's badly beaten face.

Chib continued. "The attack was savage."

Garrick stared at the images, comparing them to the dashing man on the beach. He was unrecognisable. "Assuming his wife almost cleaned him out, he maintained a decent standard of living. Nice house, car, clothes. His watch was taken..."

"Forensics say the indentation in his skin is a match for a Rolex," said Fanta, "Although they can't be too sure."

"So, he had either kept money away from his ex, or was now making a good profit on the art."

"Or both," said Harry, slowly rotating back-and-forth on his chair as he took in the wall.

Chib glanced through her notes. "He kept the house after

the divorce. She took the holiday villa and almost everything else."

Garrick stood for a closer look at the picture of Fraser's ex-wife. She was a few years younger than him. Long black hair framed high cheekbones that gave her an austere yet beguiling quality. Her necklace, earrings and bangles looked expensive.

"This was fourteen months ago? They looked happy enough. Why the sudden divorce?"

"The deceased was having an affair, which came to a head when he got her pregnant."

"He's a father?"

"Apparently. We're still trying to get in touch with the mistress. She lives in London. What are you thinking?"

Garrick was silent for a moment as he studied the picture of the smiling couple, imagining their perfect life together suddenly thrown into upheaval because of Fraser's infidelity.

"It feels too light to be a simple breaking and entering gone wrong. The owner is dead on the floor, yet the burglar didn't search the house. He took a Rolex, but never went upstairs to see if there were any more watches or jewellery. Or even money. He's a known art dealer, but the prints were left untouched on the walls. His Mercedes was left in the garage," Chib informed the team.

"What does this feel like to you?" Garrick enjoyed pushing his DS. She was smart, but still didn't have the confidence to voice her own opinions. He had never assumed that his own theories were right. Often hearing other people come up with the same ideas allowed him to see any obvious holes.

Chib thought for a moment, before registering surprise. "A revenge attack?"

"You mean the snubbed mistress?" said Wilkes in surprise.

Garrick tapped the photograph of the ex-wife. "Or the spurned lover who didn't want to see him get back on his feet."

"You said it felt like a hit," said Chib quietly. "That's still a possibility."

Garrick saw the flash of excitement between Fanta and Wilkes. As the two youngest members of the team, still in their twenties, they were still innocent enough to get excited about some of the gruesome things people did to one another.

"An assassination!" cried Fanta, with too much enthusiasm.

Garrick held up a cautionary hand. "Let's not get too far ahead of ourselves. But we need to consider it. What if he was getting roughed up for information and it got out of hand?"

"The killer panics and shoots him. Runs from the house as quickly as possible," said Chib.

"Only pausing to nick whatever he could see to make it look like a robbery gone wrong."

Silence descended as everybody contemplated the idea. Garrick felt uplifted. He thrived on having a purpose and, with everything else going on in his life, this was a welcome distraction. Even more so because the victim was a known creep, so his empathy levels were low.

"We need to find the ex-lover. Chib, London is your old stomping ground, isn't it?" She nodded. "See what you can turn up." He addressed the rest of the team. "I want to know when Rebecca was last in the country and if our man had been to see her since the divorce. And we need to speak to the gallery owner."

"On it," said Harry Lord, rising from his seat.

"No, Harry, I'm going to go. I want you to look into any criminal links he previously had and let's see if any of them were feeling particularly disgruntled towards our man."

Harry looked disappointed as he sat back down, but he nodded.

"Pepsi, you're always complaining you don't get out." Fanta threw Garrick a withering look. While he claimed to keep forgetting her name, she knew it was just a wind-up. "You're coming with me."

"You're actually letting me out of here?" Her face lit up; all snarky asides forgotten.

"Maybe you will see something in the crappy art he sells. You can educate me."

With an excited bounce in her step, Fanta snatched her jacket from the back of her seat. "I'm ready!"

"David! A word." Superintendent Margery Drury stood at the doorway and beckoned him over. Garrick wondered how long she had been there. He nodded and turned to Fanta.

"Give me a few minutes and tell me everything about the gallery on the way."

He took a couple of steps, following Drury to her office, when Chib stood in his way. She was concerned and kept her voice low.

"One thing, sir. Pathology confirms that he was beaten up before he died, but there are no defensive marks on his hands or arms." Garrick frowned. He was being assaulted, but hadn't raised his arms to ward off the blows? "And there are indications some wounds were a few days old."

"He could have been restrained. Send Wilkes to Tenterden and find out when Fraser was last seen out and about."

· · ·

DRURY'S OFFICE was overly warm, enhanced by a rare showing of the sun directly blazing through the window. There were no blinds or curtains, so when she sat behind her desk she was forced to squint.

"How're you feeling, David?"

"Absolutely fine." He declined from sitting down. He was eager to get on the road.

Drury angled away from the window, shielding her eyes from the glare, but she was stalling as she picked her words carefully. Something that was quite out of character in all the years Garrick had known his superior officer. Ordinarily she was a powerhouse who rode roughshod over people's feelings if it got the job done.

"Dr Harman seems pleased with your sessions." Garrick nodded. He couldn't think what the right response would be. "In fact, she has suggested that you would benefit from continuing them."

Garrick tried not to react. The sessions had been in place since Christmas, just after he attended Sam McKinzie's funeral, the man he had thought would become his brother-in-law. Sam was found murdered on a remote snowbound ranch in Illinois, with a few other victims and signs that Garrick's sister, Emelie, had been abducted and later killed. Therapy wasn't something he had requested or even considered, but he had found it useful. He also remembered it was only supposed to be for a couple of months.

"I'm happy either way," he said diplomatically. It would be a shame not to see Harman again, although preferably in a non-professional setting, but alarm bells were ringing. Did Drury really think she needed to keep an eye on him?

"Good," Drury said, suddenly a little more chipper. "Then let's do that. It can only be a good thing." She hesitated again, and Garrick sensed that wasn't the only issue on the table. "Especially after the incident with John Howard."

Since wrapping the case concerning murdered immigrants, several other agencies had stepped in to take control. From the National Crime Agency, who were unpicking the drug smuggling network Garrick had uncovered, through to the Military Police who were reopening John Howard's old service records since he was dishonourably discharged while serving in the Falklands Conflict. Garrick's friendship with him over the years had meant that, although he had solved the case, loose ends needed to be taken up by other detectives with no personal connection to the serial killer.

"I'm dealing with that scumbag just fine," he assured her.

Drury steepled her fingers, once again searching for her words. "I'm sure you are. It's just that you may be called upon to give evidence about him."

"Naturally."

"I mean beyond just this case."

"He's suspected in something else?"

"Early days, David. The movements of a man like him need to be thoroughly examined."

"A cold case?"

"I'm not privileged to know any details. Other than I've been asked for your cooperation, should it be required."

The energy he had been feeling minutes earlier evaporated as he dragged his heels to his car with Fanta in tow. She was talking rapidly and with more enthusiasm than he could muster. It took over an hour to make the thirty-mile drive, by which time Garrick had already forgotten half the things she had said.

5

Rye was a picturesque historical village set a couple of miles back from the Channel on the conflux of the rivers Brede and Rother. It was often cited as one of the most photographed villages in the UK. Garrick began questioning its popularity as he struggled to find a parking spot in the cramped Lucknow Place car park. He could smell the refreshing scent of the sea from here, and hungry gulls swooped overhead. The ticket machine was broken, but Fanta assured him she would pay on her phone, as long as she was reimbursed before the end of the week.

They walked down the narrow East Cliff Street as it curved onto the equally tight High Street where barely two cars could pass. The village was populated by several cafes, local souvenir shops, a traditional sweet shop and a couple of art galleries promoting local artists that all gave a distinct air of respectability to the town. Cinq Arts Gallery sat on the corner. A quaint whitewashed lower front was crowned by a distinctive crimson tiled upper story. Stepping inside dispelled any notion of old school antiquity.

Monitors hung on the walls, displaying images of rolling artwork, while ever-changing LED lights cast pools of vibrant colours across the walls. Smooth and slow contemporary drum music played over a hidden speaker system. Twisted sculptures made from stone or metal were Interspersed between the monitors. Above them hung a dozen abstract paintings. Garrick recognised two in the same style as those in Fraser's living room.

A gangly pale thirty-something, in a black tight polo neck top and jeans far too tight to be comfortable, appeared from the back. Impeccably groomed, his black hair was shaved at the side, but shot straight up by several inches in a fashion that Garrick assumed was supposed to be stylish, but he suspected it was more ironic. A single diamond earring sparkled in the mood lighting.

"Welcome!" he waved with one hand, his mobile gripped in the other. "Are you and your daughter looking for something specific?"

Garrick heard Fanta's snigger behind him. She had left her hat in the car and was wearing her police jacket, but the insignia was blocked by Garrick. He was only 41, and although DC Liu looked younger than her mid-twenties, he still couldn't pass as her adopted father. Bloody millennials. He held up his card.

"I'm DCI Garrick, this is *Officer* DC Liu," he said their names with pointed emphasis and the man's smug smile dropped. "Are you the proprietor?"

"Yes, sir. Mark Kline-Watson. How may I help… officers?"

"I believe you sell work for an art agent. Derek Fraser."

Mark nodded, but his shoulders were tense. A bead of perspiration formed on his brow. Garrick was never one to jump to immediate conclusions, especially as people became nervous and tongue-tied around cops, but he couldn't shake the feeling that their visit was expected.

"Y-yes. I sell on his behalf."

Fanta crossed to two pictures hung either side of a monitor playing fading countryside scenes.

"These two are by Hoy, right?"

Mark nodded. "Yes. That's the artist Derek is pushing hard. A wonderful talent."

Garrick looked at the paintings, both some two-foot long. One was a series of horizontal green lines, interspersed by the white of the canvas. Three circles were painted amongst them, two orange and the other blood red. The second painting had similar horizontal green lines intersected by jagged brown vertical scars.

"What are they supposed to be?" Garrick asked.

"The English countryside," Fanta replied in a tone that suggested it was obvious.

Garrick's brow furrowed as he looked harder. "I don't... what part of the countryside, exactly?"

Mark joined them; his eyes riveted on the canvases. "This is the beating heart of what makes the British landscape so iconic." He pointed to the first. "This is the Kent Downs. The spirit laid bare on the canvas. A spiritual ode of love and aspiration."

Garrick gestured to the rest of the paintings in the gallery. "Are these all Hoys?"

Fanta scoffed. "No. Can't you tell? The others don't possess this energy!"

Garrick looked at her, trying to work out if she was making fun of him or not. She was unreadable.

"To appreciate art, you need to step back." She took a physical step backwards. "Spin it around in your head." She held out her hands, fingers forming a frame which she tilted one way then the other. "Look at it from a different point of view to challenge yourself. And check out that negative space!"

Garrick looked at her as if she'd cracked. Then he turned to Mark. "People actually buy this stuff?"

Mark looked shocked. "Of course! It's art. The last Hoy sold for thirty thousand. I've earmarked these two for sixty."

It was Garrick's turn to be shocked. "You expect somebody to pay sixty grand for two pictures that look as if they have been drawn in a nursery school?"

"Each." Despite his nerves, Mark looked indignant. "Beauty is in the beholder's eye. This is especially true for art. And Derek only provides Hoy's work a couple of pieces at a time, which of course restricts the market..."

"And bumps up the value," Garrick finished.

"He was doing a Banksy with Hoy!" exclaimed Fanta.

Mark nodded. "Why not? A phantom artist captures the public's imagination."

Fanta looked appreciatively at the other pieces on display. All abstract arrays of colours and shapes. "And what did Mr Fraser sell before he discovered this wunderkind?"

"Mostly local artists. More traditional landscapes and such. Things you may approve of," he added with a sharp look in Garrick's direction.

"But his sales only really kicked off with Hoy?"

"Yes. Derek was quite savvy in the way he promotes him. And people respond."

Garrick gave up trying to find a deeper meaning in the smudges on the wall. If anything, the pictures were irritating him. "We need to speak to this Hoy. What's the full name?"

"I don't know."

"What do you mean, you don't know?"

"Derek was his agent. I never met the artist. Nobody has. That's part of the fun."

Garrick and Fanta swapped a look.

"Fraser brings in the art. You pay him the money when it sells, and that's it?"

"He doesn't even buy me dinner," Mark quipped. "Of course, I've asked to meet Hoy, but Derek is very guarded. It's his golden goose, he said."

"But there was an interview..." Garrick looked to Fanta for help. He had zoned out on the drive when she had read out the Country Life article.

"There were quotes," Mark corrected. "Which Derek sourced directly from Hoy. You'll have to ask him. Sorry, Detective, but what exactly is this all about?"

"Mr Fraser was murdered in his home yesterday."

Garrick studied Mark carefully. There was a widening of the eyes; a small backward jolt of the head, as if physically struck. Shock. Then, an unexpected chuckle of relief, which was quickly blocked when Mark covered his mouth with the back of the hand clutching the phone.

"Sorry. That must have sounded weird. That's terrible, of course. But I was worried... I thought..." he vaguely indicated to the Hoy artwork.

"Why would you think it was linked to the paintings?"

Mark scratched the back of his neck in an obvious sign of hesitation. "Because, well. They're becoming valuable."

"Who do you think would have a grudge against Mr Fraser?"

"A grudge? No one. He was garnering quite a reputation."

"And how can we get in touch with Hoy?"

Mark shrugged. "That's the question." His face suddenly

dropped as something occurred to him. Garrick read his mind.

"You've just realised he's your golden goose too. Without Fraser, how're you going to get more art to sell?"

"There is that..." he replied quietly.

Fanta spoke up. "At least you have these two here. He'll be in touch. Especially if he's expecting to sell these for over a hundred thousand pounds." Mark nodded. "And then you will put him in touch with us."

"Of course," Mark mumbled.

"I want a list of every customer you've sold work to for Mr Fraser."

"That may be difficult..." he coughed when Garrick shifted position, subtly straightening so that he loomed over the younger man. "I mean, data protection laws and all that..."

"I understand. In that case, I will come back with a warrant and formally search every nook and cranny to get them."

Mark cleared his throat. "But of course, as you are the police, I am sure I won't have any such problems if I gave them to you."

THEY WAITED A FURTHER fifteen minutes for Mark to print hard copies of each order, by which time Garrick's bad mood was deepening. When they left the gallery, he walked at such a pace that Fanta had to double-time it to keep up.

"What's the matter, sir?" Her slide back to formality indicated a worry that she'd crossed the line with her boss.

"You really admired that crap back there? A kid could have painted them!"

"No. I thought they were awful." Garrick stopped so suddenly that she almost bumped into him. "I recognised them from the magazine article," she explained quietly. "I thought it would help if he thought we had some knowledge…"

"DC Liu… that was good thinking," he admitted. They glanced back at the shop in time to see Mark switch the door sign over to 'closed'. "Tell me what you got from that little show."

"He is worried about something, but I don't think it's the murder. And that was before he realised he may lose his best-selling artist. Some of those other pieces were dire, and that's compared to the rubbish that sells. When he was printing out the invoices, I caught an email on his screen from his letting agent. It was only a glimpse, but I think he's in arrears on the shop. I suspect he's not cash fluid. Did you see his phone?"

"An iPhone. I am a Detective," he reminded her. "I get paid to spot these things."

"A two-year-old model." She chuckled when he frowned. "His skin and hair regime must take up a substantial part of his evening. A man like that is all image, Mr Metrosexual. He can't function in the social circles he orbits with a phone that is two years out of date."

"Money problems." Despite his irritation, he was impressed with her eye for detail. "That still doesn't explain what he was worried about when he realised we were police."

"Well, he deals with art, so the natural worry there would be forgery."

"But why forge an artist who is only just on the rise, and frankly, could be copied by me when I'm drunk?"

"Perhaps he owed money to Fraser or Hoy, or both."

"I want more background on our little art friend. And a

list of Fraser's next of kin. Get somebody to comb through his house for all his contacts. He must have Hoy's details copied down somewhere."

"I would keep it on my phone."

"Which we assume was stolen..." Garrick finished.

"Could that be what the thief wanted? Did he torture him to reveal Hoy's identity?"

"You watch too many movies."

A nest of motives was opening, but many centred around a phantom artist who could disappear into the ether as quickly as they arrived. And there was something else bothering Garrick. Something he was struggling to put his finger on.

By the time they returned to his Land Rover, he was furious to see a parking ticket on his windscreen. Fanta was so excited to be doing some actual work out of the office, that she had forgotten to pay for the ticket on her phone.

The rest of the trip back to the incident room was conducted mostly in silence.

6

Before they arrived back in the incident room, word came in that Fraser's only identifiable next of kin was his ex-wife and he'd left a will denying her a single penny in the event of his death. That left his child as the next in line, and the news from Chib was that they had tracked the mistress down in London, and she was going to visit her in the morning for a statement.

Back at home, Garrick showered, heated a dubious-tasting noodle ready meal in the microwave, then sat at his dining room table and removed the sheet from the fossil he'd been diligently cleaning for the last month. He had found it a relaxing, meditative experience, but over the last couple of weeks he hadn't touched the black spiralling snail shell. He'd used an air scribe, a small pneumatic needle like a miniature jackhammer, to remove the surrounding rock material. Now mostly free of the matrix that had imprisoned the evidence for millions of years, the basic shape had been revealed. With a small stainless-steel set of tools, which he'd purchased on eBay and looked more at home in a sadistic dentist's surgery, he began to clean his prize. Angling a stand-mounted magnifier so he could get a better look, he gently scraped the tiny fragments loose.

Almost two hours passed, only interrupted with thoughts on what type of creature once called this shell home. Ordinarily, he would turn to John Howard for such scholarly advice, but that was now another part of his life slammed closed.

The lovely Dr Harman had once compared his fossil restoration, not as a hobby, but as an extension of his work. Effectively, he was finding a dead body on the shore, albeit one that was millions of years old. Then the process of chipping away the deceit and lies began until the truth was revealed. Garrick had tried to point out he had a love of fossils since his schooldays, but she had been set on her analogy.

Sometimes people only see what they want to see.

Just like Hoy's paintings. All it took was one influencer to say they were groundbreaking, and the sheep would follow, paying astronomical sums of money for the privilege. Garrick was most definitely in the wrong profession.

His headache returned, perhaps from straining his eyes through the magnifier. It was a more palatable excuse than thinking it was because of the growth in his head. His consultant had prescribed co-codamol to deal with the pain, but he'd tried not to use it for fear of developing an addiction to the stuff. That was the last thing he needed. Yet the pain became unbearable, forcing him to abandon the ammonite, take the medication, and curl up in bed.

He jolted awake at four in the morning. He could have sworn the landline had woken him. Running down the stairs he saw the answerphone didn't have any message and dialling 1471 revealed the last call was three days ago from a freephone number. Shivering in his boxers and a t-shirt, Garrick was now wide awake and feeling unusually anxious. A text from Wendy had come in while he was asleep. She proposed they see a musical in Canterbury at the weekend. Garrick inwardly groaned, he couldn't think of anything worse, but she had a friend in the orchestra who could get them cheap tickets. And he was enjoying Wendy's company enough to endure two hours of somebody warbling on stage. He'll reply later. He didn't want to seem too keen.

Now wide awake, he texted Chib and told her he'd come with her to London to interview Derek Fraser's ex-mistress. He had a few early morning hours to kill before breakfast, and his headache was still there. He didn't know what to do with himself.

LONDON WAS the usual sprawling mass of lethargic traffic that Garrick didn't miss. Since moving to Kent, he had spurned big cities, and winding through the snarl in Camden was a reminder of why. He was glad Chib had offered to drive. It had given him a chance to mock her Nissan Leaf electric car, and he took great delight when she informed him they would have to find a recharge station while they conducted the interview, otherwise they wouldn't be able to make it back to Maidstone.

He decided not to mention the luxurious amount of leg space that a car with no mechanical engine offered. Nor the near-silent ride that was a blessing to his pounding head. He brought his DS up to date with the Rye gallery incident, and she told him about the progress they were making talking with Fraser's known criminal affiliates. DCs Lord and Wilkes had been tracking them down in person and had discovered a trail of bad blood.

"Although Fraser did the time for fixing up stolen cars and reselling ones that had been written off, there were rumours he had plea-bargained."

"Had he?"

Chib shrugged. "Not as far as we can tell. But some of his ex-thugs-in-arms think he spilled the beans about a group who were stealing catalytic convertors from cars, mostly while parked in driveways or public carparks. The rare elements in them sell for a fortune, and Fraser was one such trader."

"Arrests were made?"

"A few. Including Noel Benjamin."

"The name rings a bell."

"He was arrested three times for violent robberies, although they only made the last one stick. They tagged the thefts on the end of his sentence too."

"Is he still banged up?"

"In Whitemoor."

"So it couldn't be him."

"But his brother, Oscar, was the alleged brains behind those armed robberies. Nothing was ever proven, and Oscar Benjamin has no criminal record. It's generally thought his brother took the rap for him."

"What a family. Where is Oscar Benjamin now?"

"Six months ago, he sold his home in Faversham and left the country. We're trying to trace him."

Garrick never trusted coincidences. But lately, he also suspicious with neat solutions. "Keep it quiet. Let's not draw too much attention to him. I don't want him spooked."

To Garrick's chagrin, Chib found a parking space at an

electric charging point, just four-hundred-yards from their destination.

Terri Cordy lived above a betting shop on Camden High Street. She was 38, fresh-faced, despite the dark circles under her eyes, with long, mousy hair cascading down her shoulders. She answered the door wearing grey jogging slacks and a baggy black t-shirt that had seen better days. Her five-month-old son was cradled against her chest, having just gone to sleep.

The apartment was threadbare, with a battered couch that looked as if it had been retrieved from a skip, and a stained coffee table covered with the detritus of baby care. There was no television, and she owned a pre-smartphone era mobile.

Chib had spoken to her on the phone, but in soft tones she again confirmed Fraser's death. She was very good at delivering grim news.

Terri was unperturbed. "If I tell you I don't care, does that make me look guilty?"

"Did you have much contact with him?"

Terri gave a derisive snort. "Look at his mobile and tell me. He said he was going to block my calls. Then I think he did."

"Did you want child support from him?" Chib glanced at the infant now slumbering in a cot, the only new piece of furniture in the flat.

"That would've been nice. Any acknowledgement that Ethan existed would've been welcome. He cut me off the moment his wife found out about him." She nodded towards Ethan

"How long were you two seeing one another?"

"Eight months. We met at a fundraiser. I was doing some

charity work, and he was all Scottish charm. It was about four months into it when the penny dropped, and I realised he was broke."

Garrick looked up. "Broke? I thought he was doing well before the divorce?"

"His wife spent everything, and he was just playing catch-up to stay afloat. He said he hated her and wanted out. And me, I was already in love. The age difference didn't bother me. I thought he'd divorce her. I started dreaming that we actually have a future together." She drifted into an introspective silence.

Chib gave her a little time to compose her thoughts. "Then you became pregnant?"

"He was happy at first. That's what convinced me he'd leave her. I mean, all this time he was convinced she was shagging somebody else behind his back."

Garrick and Chib swapped a curious look. "His wife was having an affair?"

Terri nodded. "Yeah. Well, he was pretty sure. She spent more time in their villa than here. Suited us, as we could spend more time together."

"If he wasn't concerned about staying married, and he was broke because of her, what changed between the two of you? Why would he want to go back to her?" Garrick was mentally trying to understand the nature of their relationship but was drawing a blank.

"Good question. When he found out about *her* affair, he was the one that snapped. She was delighted to hear about us. I think it was just the excuse she was looking for."

Garrick held up his hand to interrupt. "Fraser knew *she* was having an affair, and that bothered him. But when she learned about you, she didn't care? And that bothered him more?"

"For a bit. Then he suddenly had an about-face then denied the baby was his."

"What made him doubt it?" asked Chib.

"No reason. And when Ethan was born, Derek even took a paternity test, but he didn't want to see the results. He just cut me off."

"Did he ever talk about his life before you met?"

"You mean about prison?" She nodded. "Said he was stitched up."

"By whom?"

She didn't want to answer at first. "By Oscar Benjamin."

"Did he say how or why?"

She shook her head and stared at the sleeping baby, a silent indication that line of questioning was over.

"What was he doing for money when you were together?" asked Chib.

"He was talking about setting up an antiques shop. We had a friend who had one in Islington. Derek started experimenting by selling things on eBay. He didn't have a clue, really. It was all a bunch of old tat. That's why he was at the fundraiser."

"Where you met?"

"He was looking at getting into art. That's what I studied in uni."

Garrick cocked his head. "Paintings?"

"That's where the real money is."

"Was Fraser a good artist?"

Terri snorted. "He was terrible. Fancied himself as one. Kept talking about doing a course, but he was talentless."

"What do you know about an artist named Hoy?"

Terri laughed and rose to check on the baby. "That happened after he dumped me. We used to go to art fairs and exhibitions. He was always on the lookout for new talent. Never found it."

"We need to get in touch with Hoy," said Chib.

Terri tightened the blanket around the baby. "Good luck. But I don't have a clue. I'll be honest with you. I don't care that he's dead. The bastard had it coming. Don't think for a second that I'm the only one he has ever kicked in the teeth and walked away from. My only interest is what he left us." She looked at the two officers. "Which I'm guessing is nothing." She gestured around. "He left us in squalor. I can't afford childcare. I can't go back to work. And he didn't care."

Garrick stood, his knees cracking from the effort. He felt sorry for Terri. She was one of the ignored victims of such crimes. A loose end that could never be tied up. Given nothing and left with less.

"That's a matter for the solicitors to sort out, I'm afraid." He moved to her side and looked at the sleeping baby. "Did he never attempt to see him?"

"He never tried. Never asked. He stopped responding to all my messages. Just cut me from his life entirely. I'm one of these people that is never given an explanation. I'm just expected to let life trample over me and be happy about it."

7

"**D**etective Garrick, can you comment further on the murder of Derek Fraser?"

Garrick wasn't expecting the double flash from the SLR to burst so close to his face. The sudden white light felt like needles in his eyeballs, provoking a migraine like Vesuvius erupting in his skull.

"Is it true he was shot?" The young reporter thrust her phone closer, recording every word. She had bobbed red hair, a swatch of freckles across her cheeks and nose, and the most intense green eyes he'd seen. Another three men flanked her. One was a reporter he recognised, the other was his video cameraman.

"No comment," Garrick said automatically, favouring the video camera.

"What about tortured?" pressed the well-informed redhead.

Garrick's hesitation made her smile knowingly. This wasn't how he had expected his lunchtime run to Pret to develop. He had simply wanted a break from the cloying atmosphere in the incident room, and a chance to exchange a few messages with Wendy.

"The pathologist hasn't yet released his report." It was an evasive 'yes,' and they both knew it.

"His death is rocking the local art world. Do you think it is linked to the rise of Hoy's popularity?"

Rocking the art world? That was news to Garrick.

"We're exploring all options," he replied, stepping around the reporter and into the station. Before he could make it to the office, Drury blocked his path.

"Reporters have been calling all morning. The BBC has been chasing your case. They wanted you down the studio for South East Today. I declined on your behalf."

Television interest was either a sign of a slow-news day, or the reporter outside hadn't been exaggerating how the art world was responding.

"We're going to have to give then something soon," Drury continued, "So I want a full debriefing on where you're at by the end of the day."

Stepping into the incident room, Garrick was greeted by stressful expressions from Fanta and DC Sean Wilkes. Wilkes was on a call; Fanta was surfing the internet. She caught Garrick's look.

"Before you ask, it's work. He's gone viral." She angled the screen so he could see a Twitter page. Garrick avoided social media, and although he was a spritely young man when the internet had boomed, he'd actively avoided it as just another fad.

"Why?" He dropped his paper sandwich bag on his desk and took his coat off. "And just how bad is that?"

"It turns out Fraser was the only connection to Hoy. He - or she - is the one who's gone viral, really. A secret artist wrapped up in a murder, well, that's just got everybody excited. People are already asking for more of his work. It's going to drive the price up."

"Christ. Any luck searching the house for contact details?"

Wilkes hung up the phone. "No, sir. I was with uniform at the house yesterday and we opened every book and piece of paper we could find. Nothing. No sign of a mobile or laptop either."

"And Fraser's buyers?"

"Just got off the phone from the last one. He'd sold about six Hoys before the last one flew off the shelf for just a couple of hundred. I tell you, Fraser must have had had a good PR spin to push the price up to thirty grand. Now the other owners are all rubbing their hands with glee. None of them met either Fraser or Hoy. Fraser was strictly a middleman. Art to gallery. Money to him."

"Bank details?"

"That's where it gets interesting," Fanta chimed up. "All payments from Mark Kline-Watson were made to an account in Panama."

"Wonderful. Always naturally helpful, Panoramian bankers."

"*Panoramian?* Is that an actual thing?"

"What else would they be called?"

"I'm sure it's Panamanian. Are you thinking of Pomeranian? That's a type of dog, I think."

"Whatever you call them, throw everything we can at them for details, but don't hold your breath. What about former criminal liaisons?"

"Harry is still doing the rounds. On the whole, they're all

delighted Fraser got what they thought he deserved. And they all have watertight alibis."

He looked up as Chib entered with a scowl. "What happened to you?"

"I was ambushed outside. Have you seen the reporters?"

"There were a couple."

"There's more at the car park gate. They're multiplying."

"Not enjoying the limelight, Chib?"

She sat at her desk and pulled a face as she logged on to the computer.

Ignoring them, Fanta continued. "Border Force came back with details on Oscar Benjamin. He's been back and forth to Portugal every few months and stays for a few days. He's in the UK now. Arrived in Gatwick two weeks ago."

"Portugal? Same as the ex." He saw the look on Chib's face. She was thinking the same thing. "Did Oscar run off with Mrs Fraser? Do we have an address for Oscar Benjamin?"

"No. We're looking out for him."

Garrick clasped his hands behind his head and stretched his shoulders back with a satisfying crack. He looked at the evidence board. It was now filled with pictures of anybody linked to Fraser. Most were taken from social media.

"To summarise, we currently have one dead body. An artist we can't trace. An alleged criminal who might be sleeping with his ex, but who we can't yet find, and whose brother is in prison. Which rules him out. The ex-wife's in another country and the ex-girlfriend who is delighted to see him dead, but she has an alibi."

Everybody fell silent.

"That leaves us with an art dealer who has everything to gain," said Fanta. Everybody turned to look at her. "He called earlier. Those two Hoys sold this morning. A hundred grand each."

Garrick's jaw slackened. "What's his commission on that?"

"Thirty per cent." She saw Garrick's lips moved as he calculated. "Sixty thousand British Pounds," she clarified.

"I wonder how much of that Fraser gets to pocket?"

"Still waiting on his bank records," said Chib. "Then we'll know."

The rest of the afternoon resulted in a quick message exchange with Wendy, confirming Saturday was going to be a splendid night at the theatre, with a few drinks beforehand. Their previous dates had been slow but fun. He'd taken each one with no expectations. This was the first time he was looking forward to one, despite the fact they were seeing a musical called '*Curtains*'.

The end-of-day deadline for Drury's update was looming when the final forensics report from Fraser's house came in. Chib read it in silence for several minutes, thoughtfully tapping her lips with her index finger before Garrick prompted her.

"Is that the next Dan Brown you have there?"

Fanta threw him a look. "Who's he?"

Chib pointed to the report. "They only found Fraser's prints around the house. They're all logged on IDENT1 from when he did time." The UK's national fingerprint database housed everybody's biometrics data if they had had a brush with the law. "Nobody else's."

"So the killer was very careful. This sounds more premeditated than a spur-of-the-moment B&E."

"There's a lot of DNA evidence in the living room. Well, hair."

"Do we have a match?"

"Nothing on record. But isn't that strange? The killer probably wore gloves, but not a hat. It's the most obvious DNA to leave behind, so it seems odd to me."

Garrick sighed. "So far, we are telling the press that we are looking for a man without a hat. Well, that certainly limits the scope of the investigation."

DC Harry Lord's return to the office confirmed more dead ends.

"Nobody was unhappy to hear that Derek Fraser is dead. Everybody has alibis. The only thing I could confirm was that he owed Oscar Benjamin money. A quarter of a million was mentioned a few times."

"That's a lot of money."

Harry nodded. "As far as I can work out, it was lent to him for the car dealership, which is why Fraser moved into petty crime after he did his time, so that he could pay him back. There was talk that they'd met up a few times to work out the debt, but again, nobody is sure."

Garrick was thoughtful. "It would be handy to have a link between Oscar Benjamin and that account in Panama."

"Panama?" Lord looked around the room. "Have I missed something?"

"Nothing gets past your radar, does it Harry? Although, I wouldn't mind a brew."

Harry sighed. He hadn't even got his jacket off before being demoted to tea boy.

IT WAS six o'clock on the dot when Superintendent Margery Drury entered the incident room and demanded an update. The very short presentation was greeted with crossed arms and a deepening vertical furrow between her brows.

"I have to say," she finally said, "in my whole career, that has to be about the briefest briefing I have ever heard. No witnesses. No strong suspects. No motive."

"We have hair follicles at the crime scene, which I bet match Oscar Benjamin. I would say that's very compelling. And if we track him down by the end of the evening–" Fanta added hopefully.

Garrick halted her unrealistic expectations. "If he is the killer, then he's smart enough to go to ground."

"Although it is rather convenient," muttered Chib.

Garrick threw her a look. "Chib–"

"DS Okon, why is that?"

Chib shifted uncomfortably in her seat as Drury focused her impatient wrath on her. She glanced at Garrick, who rubbed his temple and shook his head. The pain from lunchtime's migraine was still wearing him down.

"The follicles were only in the living room, around the body. Nowhere else."

"Because they struggled," said Garrick. "Which is why he was shot."

"But why didn't the killer look around the house?"

Garrick held up his hands; he didn't know. "There was no time. After the gunshots he lost his bottle and ran. Or his hat got knocked off in the struggle, then he put it back on."

"Ah, so we're now looking for a man *with* a hat," said Fanta with a grin – which vanished when Drury fixed her with a looked that sucked any joy from the room. She raised a finger, as if addressing a higher power.

"As we speak, I believe the murder is the lead story on the Six O'clock News. Newsnight requested you," she looked pointedly at Garrick. "It seems your reputation from the John

Howard affair is carrying some notoriety. They even believe that you are a competent police detective."

DC Harry Lord chose the wrong time to snigger. He looked away when Drury swept her gaze across the room.

"I want you to draft a statement with Communications. Something that tells everybody about the great strides we're making but gives no details because of operational purposes. Especially as we don't have any."

"Why don't we throw a press conference?" said Garrick as the idea struck him.

"I'm not in the frame of mind for you to take the piss, David."

"I'm serious, ma'am." He hopped to his feet and crossed to the evidence wall. He tapped Oscar Benjamin's photo. "He's our prime suspect. He arrived in the country recently, but we've been unable to locate him. I bet once we collar him, we'll be able to match his DNA to the scene. And there is plenty of animosity between the two men to work out a motive. Find Oscar Benjamin and we crack this case. That's the whole pitch. If the media are this interested, then let's use them to our advantage for a change. We'll use the press to smoke him out."

8

It was the worst idea Garrick could remember having, and it was made worse by Drury's sudden enthusiasm, especially as Garrick would have to front it. During the drive home, he missed two calls from Wendy. He messaged her back with an excuse that he was busy with work. As the case was on his mind, it wasn't an untruth.

The team had stayed late preparing the slides needed for the presentation, which was set for lunchtime the next day at Maidstone Town Hall. Garrick had secretly hoped some crucial piece of evidence would come to light so they could cancel the event, but he wasn't holding his breath.

He tasked DC Liu with talking to Mark Kline-Watson again with the aim to dig into the details of his relationship with Fraser. The gallery owner was already under strict instructions not to move the money from the art sale. He was more than happy to keep it in his account for as long as possible. He had also lamented that demand for more Hoys were now coming in thick and fast.

While he couldn't fault Chib's case against Oscar

Benjamin, Garrick felt that Mark Kline-Watson must be involved too. It was the old police vibe of being nothing more than a hunch, so he decided not to share it with the rest of the team until something substantial emerged.

Sure enough, Derek Fraser and the mysterious artist were the lead story on Newsnight. Garrick watched with morbid curiosity as the focus on the report leaned towards the mysterious artist's identity rather than the brutal murder. He was sure that this was a good sounding board for how the press conference would unfold tomorrow.

MAIDSTONE TOWN HALL was a neoclassical design, with a solid white Portland stone ground floor. The second floor was adorned with large, splendid windows set amongst the red brickwork. It would have been an impressive construction in 1763. Now it looked as if somebody had dropped a stone ship between High Street and Bank Street. The Union Jack that was hoisted on a rooftop mast hung limp and wet in the current downpour.

Inside, the old courtroom's Rococo ceiling had been beautifully preserved, and was a hidden highlight, or indeed the only highlight, for the council meetings that usually occurred inside. The police Communications team were setting up a table, with Kent Police banners erected behind. Garrick watched them diligently assembling the set, while in the corner a technician was struggling to convince a large wheel-mounted television to talk to the laptop that would display the images needed during the conference.

The activity was a shelter from the outside world. Not only from the heavy downpour which looked set to remain for the day, but from the growing pool of reporters braving the elements outside the police station. The redhead had intercepted Garrick when he arrived, and he finally caught her name: Molly Meyers, from Kent Online. Hardly a national mover and shaker, but still an important liaison between the police and the good folk of the county. This time, Garrick wasn't caught off guard and gave what he hoped was a charming smile, assuring her she would hear everything at the conference. Then he impulsively added that she could have the first question. He didn't know what had made him say that.

"Detective Garrick?"

Garrick turned to see a man in a long black trench coat, dripping water all over the parquet floor. In his late fifties, with a greying beard and craggy face, he conveyed the air of a well-liked uncle.

"Yes?"

"DCI Oliver Kane. Met Police." Garrick nodded. "Do you have a few minutes to talk about John Howard?"

The man's demeanour was friendly, but the timing of the request raised Garrick's hackles. He gestured around.

"You can see I am a tad busy with a press conference."

"I just have a few questions."

"Questions that couldn't be emailed or discussed at a convenient time on the phone? Instead, you came all the way from London to ask me a 'few'?"

DCI Kane bared his teeth in a loud laugh that echoed in the hall. "Well, that would be too convenient, wouldn't it? I was in the area and knew exactly where to pin you down. Lucky for me, because I'm guessing that you are running here, there, and everywhere with this murder investigation."

"Yes. I'm quite strapped for time..."

"How long had you known Mr Howard?"

"Since I moved to Kent. Twelve years. He had that book-shop in Wye, which is how I got to know him. I believe that was in my report."

"And you were close friends?"

"Friends. As to how close, well I suppose the answer would be quite telling in the fact he concealed his homicidal tendencies from me." He gave a laugh, almost mimicking Kane's own jollity.

"Indeed. I have to say, I am most impressed with the fact you exposed him at all, and all the other crimes you uncovered... impressive. I'd tip my hat if I wore one. But just so I understand, how close did you think you were? Personally. From your point of view?"

"It's not closeness. He was intelligent. Useful. You're talking about a man who had a broad expanse of knowledge. In several previous cases he'd proved to be a good sounding board. He had a natural way of illuminating points we'd overlooked."

"You regularly discussed active cases with him?"

"He was more a consultant, I suppose."

"And expert on the criminal mind, so it turned out," Kane laughed again. "And in your case, he was a purveyor of misinformation."

"Very much so." Garrick was distracted as one of the backing boards behind the table toppled noisily over. He didn't need the set crumbling before the eyes of the national news.

"What makes you think he hasn't done that before?"

"Done what?"

"You said that you've consulted with him over many cases–"

"Consulted wasn't the right word–"

"I just wonder how many of those cases he could have seeded with misinformation?"

"None. He wasn't personally involved with those. We closed many of them."

"Many. Not all."

"DCI Kane, I'd tip my cap to you and your hundred per cent track record... if either of us had one." Kane was officially pissing him off now, and Garrick wasn't in the mood to be toyed with.

"You said you were in the area? Why? He lived above his shop and it burned down, save the shed. And forensics went over that multiple times. What is there left to look at?"

"It turns out he may have had a lockup that you didn't know about."

"Where?"

Kane tilted his head and raised his eyebrows. "It's an active investigation. You understand. And to confirm, you didn't know about this, or any other property that Mr Howard may have had?"

"No."

"Regular acquaintances? Family?"

"He mentioned a brother once. But I think he passed away. His parents too."

"And relationships...?"

"I sometimes thought he was gay, possibly. But every now and again he would produce a girlfriend he'd date for a short while. Nothing ever serious."

"Do you remember any of them? Have any pictures?"

"We were not the type of friends who holidayed together. Going out to lunch was enough."

"And did you every introduce him to your family, friends, or work colleagues?"

"My social circle is best defined as a dot. And he was it. He never came out to any police booze-ups. You know how wild they can get," he added with pointed irony. "Although he met my DS a few times when we quizzed him for advice. Other than that, no."

"DS Eric Wilson?"

Garrick nodded. He and Eric Wilson had always got on and had stayed in touch when he'd taken compassionate leave over his sister's murder. Over that period, Wilson had been seconded to Staffordshire. He'd meant to call him, and had even emailed him, but Wilson hadn't replied. That was the nature of the job. Often it sucked your personal life away into a vacuum.

"And your sister?"

"Pardon?" Garrick was aware he'd zoned out for a moment, lost in his own thoughts.

"Are you okay?" Kane studied him with concern.

"Yes." Garrick spat the word a little too harshly. His medical files were kept even from his superior officer, so there was no reason to defend himself from a Met detective who felt he was superior to his colleagues who worked out in the sticks.

"I asked if he ever met your sister?"

"A few times. What's that got to do with anything? I barely saw my sister. We didn't exactly hit it off. When she came to visit, I think once we swung by his shop to pick something up. Another time he took us out for lunch. But that was early last year. No, longer than that. The year before. It was a wholly unremarkable event."

DCI Kane watched as the stage backing board was fixed upright. He glanced at his watch. "I suppose I best leave you to it. I always get nervous before these things."

Garrick felt relieved to see Chib enter, bone dry as she shook an umbrella in the doorway. He hadn't been feeling nervous, but the encounter with DCI Kane had thrown him off-kilter.

"Be seeing you," Kane said with a smile as he walked away.

"Of course. And Oliver," Garrick took some satisfaction to see the first-name cause a flicker of annoyance across Kane's face. "Any time you have questions, day or night, please don't hesitate to email me."

Kane gave a small smile and turned away, pointedly ignoring Chib as he passed her.

Chib sized Garrick up with a frown. "You okay, sir? You look as if you haven't slept all night."

GARRICK AND CHIB stood in a side room as the main hall filled with reporters. He counted nine television cameras, complete with assorted reporters. Microphones with BBC, SKY and ITV logos were flashed like status badges. He was surprised to see CNN, ABC, France 24 and an Al Jazeera logo amongst them too. An army of at least another thirty reporters and photographers increased the ranks. He'd once asked DC Harry Lord if there was a collective noun for reporters. Harry suggested it had to be a *Bastard of Press*.

"Bloody hell. It looks like the entire world is out there," Garrick muttered to Chib.

For once, her confident demeanour was shaken, and she looked ready to throw up.

"Are you sure you need me out there, sir?" she said in a weak voice.

"Pull yourself together, Chib. You'll be fine. They want a

story. We want them to find Oscar Benjamin. As long as our
I.T. doesn't crash, this is nothing more than a dog and pony
show. Follow my lead, you'll be fine." His smile provoked one
in response, although inside, he was feeling just as nervous.

The door opened and a young woman from the Communications team popped her head around.

"Everybody's ready if you are?"

Garrick pulled a piece of paper from his suit pocket and
unfolded it. It was a series of bullet points the team had
agreed on the night before. He noticed Fanta had kindly
labelled the list 'Idiot Points'.

His mouth felt dry, but Garrick nodded. He'd done
dozens of conferences in the past and cursed DCI Kane for
getting him worked up. They entered the hall and walked the
few yards to the table that now had a sheet draped over it
with the Kent Police logo hanging in the centre: a white Kent
horse rampant in a red circle, surrounded by a blue ring. The
same logo was on the television that the technician had
finally got working.

Silence descended on the room, broken only by a
constant ripple of clicks from the flanks of SLRs. Lights
erected to help the cameras, made Garrick squint and he felt
uncomfortable under the heat they generated. The glare
niggled his headache, which until then, had remained merci-
fully subdued. He noticed Molly Meyers at the front of the
pack and spotted DCI Kane lurking at the back of the hall.
Apparently, he wasn't in such a hurry to leave after all.

He and Chib took their seats. He glanced at the Communications woman who stood at the side and she held up a
small remote clicker, ready to advance the presentation.
Garrick angled the gooseneck microphone on the table as
Chib poured them both a glass of water, which sounded

overly loud so close to the mic. He placed the idiot notes in front of him and swept his gaze across the reporters, trying not to linger on any one television camera.

"Thank you all for coming," Garrick began.

He didn't need the notes. He worked on autopilot as he outlined the general condition they'd found Derek Fraser in. As agreed, he played up Fraser's big loss to the art world and stressed that the mysterious Hoy must get in touch with the police as soon as possible. He added that the artist's last two works had just sold for one hundred and twenty grand, reasoning that if Hoy didn't know about the sale, then the sum of money owed to him would certainly give him cause to pick up the phone.

The images of Derek Fraser, smiling with his ex-wife, and the ones taken for his Country Life article, appeared on cue on the TV. They'd been especially chosen to show the friendly nature of the deceased to elicit sympathy. Finally, the images of Oscar Benjamin's scowling face came up, taken from a time he had been brought in for questioning. They were selected to make him look like the definitive bad guy. DS Okon took over, requesting that if the public see him, they should call 999 straight away. Garrick had convinced Chib that Joe Public would prefer to be told what to do from her, rather than a stuffy middle-aged white man.

Before he knew it, the briefing was rolling to an end. All they had to do was survive the inevitable barrage of questions. He pointed at Molly.

"We'll take a few questions, and I believe the young lady there has the first."

Molly beamed with pride, holding out her phone to capture the best audio recording she could.

"Thank you, DCI Garrick. Is there any evidence that connects Derek Fraser to–?"

"WHAT THE HELL IS GOING ON?" boomed an angry Scottish voice from the back of the room.

A murmur of consternation rose through the bank of reporters as a figure pushed his way around them and made his way to the tables. Garrick rose to confront the wet and bedraggled stranger – but the words failed him.

It was Derek Fraser.

"What's all this I hear about being dead?" Fraser demanded in a stark Scottish brogue. He looked around the room in confusion.

Cameras went crazy as they recorded the spectacle – but the Bastard of Press were all too shocked to throw out a question. Molly Meyers was the first to manage it.

"If you're not dead... then who is?"

9

G arrick had hoped to gain extensive press coverage. But not like this. Within the hour, the department was swamped with calls and a growing platoon of journalists was milling outside.

The walk to the incident room with Derek Fraser turned into a scrum, with uniformed officers providing a protective entourage as questions were yelled from every direction. Fraser looked confused and kept shouting: *"I'm very much alive, thank you!"* He took refuge in an interview room and was given a milky tea as they waited for his solicitor to join them. When she finally arrived, Rosamund Hellberg, expressed shock at the swelling crowd outside. In her fifties, with neatly curled short grey hair, Hellberg was the image of elegance and expense.

"Mr Fraser, where have you been?" As an opening gambit, Garrick knew it was poor, but he was still coming to terms with events. Chib sat next to him, hands clasped together and staring at Fraser as if he was a ghost.

"In a retreat. And the first thing I bloody hear when I get

out is that I'm dead! That's a damn shocking thing to be told. And they told me *after* I paid me bill. Which feels kinda insulting. The damage all this will do to me reputation..." he shook his head in despair. "I can't imagine putting a figure on it."

"I dare say this is doing nothing but enhancing your reputation."

Fraser pointed at Garrick. "You can't go around telling the world somebody's dead and not expect consequences."

"Really? Worse ones than actually being dead?"

"Aye!" He pointed at Garrick and looked to his solicitor. "This is defamation of character, isn't it?"

Hellberg tactfully remained silent.

"Well, I am delighted to see you are alive, and very vocal," said Garrick with forced jollity. His inner voice was screaming for answers. "I must admit, we were struggling to find a credible suspect for the murder."

Fraser held his hands palm up. "Well, I'm here. Right in front of you."

"I can see. And was that an admission of guilt?"

Fraser froze as his arrogant swagger hit pause.

"What now?"

Hellberg cut in. "My client is admitting nothing, Detective, as you well know. He was using a common expression to indicate he is alive and well. Which is something the police seem to struggle to establish."

"But somebody isn't alive and well. Somebody was brutally murdered in your house. And if it's not you, then who is it?"

"How the bloody hell should I know?" He looked at Hellberg again. "Can you believe this crap? Somebody breaks into mc house when I'm away and he's pointing fingers!"

"Mr Fraser, pointing fingers is a large part of my job." He wagged a finger at Fraser. "See? It takes years of training."

"You thought he was me. Did he look anything like me?"

Chib slid several pictures from the crime scene across the desk. Fraser picked them up, closely examining each. He passed one to Hellberg, who gave the smallest of frowns.

"Hardly an exact likeness."

"The victim's face was badly smashed with a hammer. Then he was executed with two gunshots to the chest."

Fraser was shaken as he tossed the pictures back on the desk. "So that carpet is buggered too."

Garrick watched him carefully. "You hardly seem concerned about the dead man."

"Concerned about somebody breaking into me home? No, not really."

"Do you live alone, Mr Fraser?"

"Aye."

"When were you last at home?"

"Three days ago. I left in the morning to go to Wales."

"The day of the killing."

"He wasn't there when I left. I would've noticed." Fraser crossed his arms, his defiance seeping back.

"It was actually the next day when an Amazon delivery driver found the body."

"I still wasn't there."

"Then who killed him?"

"Maybe the delivery driver did it? Ever think of that? Or... or another thief. What made you think it was me?"

Chib tapped the photo. "He is wearing your clothes, isn't he?"

"Look similar."

"He was in your house."

"He broke in."

"Your DNA was all over him."

"I do live there. It is me house."

Chib nodded, but she had clearly exhausted her line of reasoning.

"Mr Fraser, with all that evidence in hand, it does rather point the finger in your direction." He mimicked Fraser's earlier finger pointing.

"That is ridiculous," Hellberg cut in. "My client willingly entered your terrible excuse for a press conference to stop you from making a mistake. Not only was he in a retreat in Wales, and isolated from the news, you now throw unsubstantiated accusations at him with no evidence. His DNA was at the crime scene? In his own house? I am appalled you would even mention that."

Chib hung her head. Garrick was becoming increasingly annoyed.

"Then you are overlooking the one piece of evidence we have." He forcibly tapped a photograph. "The corpse down the morgue!"

"And *who* is he?" Hellberg goaded him with a cocked eyebrow.

"Obviously, that's what we need to establish."

Hellberg gathered her case and stood up. "In that case, we are done here."

"You can't go..."

"I assure you, we can. And we are. Come on," she nudged Fraser, who stood up, slightly bewildered.

"I guess we are," he said with a shrug.

"I want to talk to you about Oscar Benjamin."

Fraser paused. "What's to tell?"

"You owed him money. And until an hour ago, I was

about to accuse him of your murder."

"Well, I don't owe him shit. And I don't want to see him, ever. And I am sure the scum bag is responsible for somebody's murder. Just not mine."

"When did you last see him?"

"I can't remember. Why don't you ask Rebecca? She's sleeping with him. Why do you think we got a divorce?"

"Mr Fraser, you don't have to answer any of this." Hellberg gave Garrick a withering look. "I suggest you issue an apology to the press and stop hounding my client with false accusations."

"I'll need full details of this retreat you were on."

"I shall send them to you," Hellberg said. "Good day, Detectives."

She ushered a grinning Fraser from the room.

"God, I felt like I was back in boarding school," muttered Chib. "As much as I hate to say this, but what if he is telling the truth?"

"Then somebody is trying to set him up."

"Who?"

Garrick could think of only two people. Mark Kline-Watson and Oscar Benjamin. The man they still needed to find, but Garrick suspected that their plea to locate him will have been swamped by Fraser's rise from the dead. He wasn't wrong.

By the time they returned to the incident room, Fanta confirmed that the footage of Derek Fraser crashing the conference had gone viral worldwide. It was also playing on every channel. A text from Wendy declared:

I've just seen you on TV!

And as Drury entered the room, he knew he and his team were in for the biggest bollocking of his career.

10

The clinical white light erased almost every shadow from the morgue. The corpse, formerly known as Derek Fraser, lay on the slab. An elderly bespectacled coroner, who had the mannerisms of a timid priest, and gave every sign that he was unhappy with his job, spoke so softly that Garrick had to strain to hear. He pulled the white sheet from the face and upper body and carefully folded it across the chest, taking a little too long to ensure there wasn't a single crease.

Chib stiffened slightly, although her expression was mostly hidden behind her mask. Garrick wasn't sure how many victims she had seen, but in the short time they'd been together, she'd composed herself with cool aplomb. He put her reaction down to the smell that lingered around a several-day old corpse, which the room's extractor fans were struggling to remove.

"We should have a full DNA analysis from the lab in the morning," the Coroner said reverently.

The press was already asking questions about how the

body could have been confused with Fraser from the very beginning. Despite their assumptions, testing a victim's DNA was not an automatic response if other factors provided identification. There had been no reason to suspect the corpse was anybody else other than Derek Fraser.

Garrick cleared his throat. "We are working on the assumption that the victim broke into the house dressed, for whatever reason, as Mr Fraser."

The Coroner raised an eyebrow. "That is an unusual assumption."

"Since lunchtime, this has been an unusual case. It's possible he was deliberately wearing the clothes to pass himself off as Fraser..."

As Garrick had feared, the request for the public to be on the lookout for Oscar Benjamin had been lost in the white noise of sensationalism. Garrick was still convinced that he had a hand in the murder of... whoever was lying on the slab.

"I sent samples of the clothing to the lab as you requested," said the Coroner reading the results from a printout. "The washing detergent on the clothing matches the one found in the house. But then again, it's a common brand. However, it didn't erase all traces from the clothing. Mr Fraser's DNA was found on the inside of the trousers and shirt."

"So, they were his clothes?" said Garrick in surprise. "The victim was wearing Fraser's own clothing?"

"Indeed," the Coroner said, re-reading the results.

"Weird, but it doesn't help answer the question of why he was there though."

"Perhaps as a decoy?" said Chib. "If Fraser knew somebody was out for him. Maybe he paid a lookalike as bait?"

"There is a little more to it than that," said the Coroner. He used his little finger to indicate to the swollen face. "The damage here around the forehead, ocular orbits, and cheek-bones was inflicted with a hammer, like this one." He wheeled over a small steel table, on which were several items. He picked up a heavy claw hammer. He gently matched the round hammer head to a slight indentation in the cheek-bone. It was a perfect fit. "It was used to disfigure the face at key points, such as the cheeks. And it was done with some precision."

"To deliberately make facial ID impossible?" asked Garrick.

"That would be my thought. The victim has the same eye colour as Mr Fraser, but the hair. Look here, it has been dyed."

"Dyed?"

"To match Mr Fraser's."

Chib and Garrick exchanged a look.

"Your bait idea may not be so mad after all," said Garrick.

"These wounds are twenty hours older than the gunshots. Give or take four hours." He handed the hammer to Garrick and indicated to the claw. "That was used to intentionally damage several teeth, so a dental ID would be unreliable."

"There were no signs of torture in the house," Chib pointed out.

"He was tortured elsewhere. Then taken to the house. Then killed."

The Coroner consulted a chart. "I found substantial traces of gamma-Hydroxybutyric acid in his system."

Garrick frowned. "GHB?" He noticed Chib's confusion. "It was a popular date-rape drug in the nineties."

"And with the concentrations in him, he would have been unconscious for some time. When, or if, he came around, his recollection would have been heavily impaired."

"Not the ideal state to question him. Maybe the attacker wasn't fully aware of the side effects?"

The Coroner diligently slid the sheet lower, positioning it just above the man's groin. The revealed hairy stomach could have been politely described as a muffin top. He indicated a red welt cutting around the body.

"This was caused by his trousers being too tight. I haven't been given Mr Fraser's measurements, but they were not the same size. The trousers were too small around his waist by an inch at least, and when I removed them, I noticed that this man is at least an inch and a half taller than Mr Fraser." He moved to the corpse's left side and used his pinkie to indicate to the watch strap indentation still moulded into the dead skin. "He was wearing a watch so tightly that it would have cut off his circulation."

Garrick's head was now pounding. The brilliant lighting was stirring a migraine. "There were no bloodstains on his clothing, other than the gunshot wounds?"

"Correct."

"Then he put the clothes on after the initial assault."

"In the condition he was in, somebody dressed him. He couldn't have done it himself. He was alive, but I doubt he was conscious. And he certainly wasn't conscious when he was shot."

"Are you sure?"

"Certain. There are no defensive wounds on his hands or arms. No sign that he was restrained during any of the attacks."

"You're saying that everything was inflicted on him when he was unconscious?"

"I would say that is highly likely. This wasn't torture. At least, not as we consider it."

． ． ．

THE MORTUARY CAR park was poorly illuminated, and the rain had stopped as a hazy fog formed. Garrick and Chib walked back to their separate vehicles, dragging their feet as they worked through possible outcomes.

"Fraser must have known he was being targeted, and this poor bloke was dragged in at the last moment to take the fall," said Garrick.

"If he was passing himself off as Fraser, then he was abducted and tortured for information he obviously wouldn't know about."

"Such as the identity of a valuable artist."

Chib looked at him in surprise. "You think this is about Hoy?"

"Nobody knows who he is. Fraser conveniently disappears on a retreat the same day this fella turns up dead in his house, dressed in his clothes."

"And the killer tried to set up the scene like a burglary gone wrong."

"Yeah..." it sounded weak to Garrick, but the evidence was stacking.

"What use is it torturing him if the victim is unconscious?"

"We need to look into the movements of the gallery owner, Kline-Watson. He's a lot to gain from knowing Hoy's identity."

"Fanta said his rent was in arrears. If his business was struggling, I could see Hoy would be a perfect solution."

Garrick nodded. "And after spending a few minutes in Fraser's company, I can see he isn't the sort of person who likes to share. I can also see why somebody would want to bump him off." He looked sharply at Chib. "I didn't say that of course."

Chib blinked in surprise. "Didn't hear a thing, sir." She noticed he was acting more uptight than usual. "Are you okay?"

"Rattled, Chib. I'm rattled."

Chib glanced through an email on her phone. "It turns out Fraser's alibi checks out. He was in Wales the day before the murder. The hotel owner remembers he was quite reserved until it came to paying the bill."

"Fancy him kicking up a stink. What was this 'retreat', anyway?"

"Oh, you'll love it. It was a spiritual art getaway. According to the website, it's a chance for participants to expand their own artistic skills with the group, or to find contemplation within the countryside in order to open up one's connection with a higher power."

"I didn't realise our Mr Fraser was so spiritual."

"It was out near Hay-on-Wye. Powys police asked the participants about him. Seems he chose the countryside reflections as he didn't socialise. Kept himself to himself. When he checked out he was effing and blinding, as the hotel manager recalls."

They neared their cars parked side-by-side. Chib's Nissan Leaf was the epitome of modernism and the future; Garrick's dirty old Land Rover... he didn't need to finish that mental analogy. He was feeling it each day.

The Nissan lit up and unlocked as Chib approached. Garrick had to jiggle the key in his door several times before the central locking allowed him entrance. He paused.

"How did he get there?"

"A taxi picked him up when he left. So, I assume by train."

"I imagine it's not the easiest place to get to, and he had a perfectly nice car in the garage. One that could have made the trip there and back on a single tank of petrol," he added pointedly.

"He's been asking when he can return to his home."

"He'll have to wait. It's still a crime scene even if he is alive."

"His solicitor's been demanding we allowed him to pick up some clothes and essentials at least."

Garrick thoughtfully drummed his fingers on the car roof. "Let's get full coverage of where Mark Kline-Watson was over the last few days. I want a whole timeline of his association with Fraser and Hoy. We're missing something..."

"Probably, but what?"

"A connection between our gallery owner and Oscar Benjamin."

"You still think he's the killer?"

"He's in the mix somewhere. The affair. The debt. The fact he has gone missing."

"But he would have clearly known the difference between Fraser and somebody doubling as him."

"True. We're talking about a man who let his brother take the fall for something people claim he was responsible for. He's not the sort of man to get his hands dirty. Others do that for him. Others who wouldn't know they have killed the wrong man if they've never met him before."

Garrick's drive home was hampered by thickening fog. The concentration needed to drive didn't help his throbbing head. The news on the radio led with the story of Fraser's dramatic rise from the grave. Garrick switched it off as it cut to an interview with Derek Fraser. He knew that the canny Scotsman was milking his time in the spotlight.

Several text messages from Wendy said how much she was looking forward to their theatre trip. That was a welcome distraction, but it didn't last long. Garrick knew that the media fervour surrounding the case would only worsen if he couldn't give the lions some meat. His team needed to find *something* that would break the case soon.

He didn't know that it was about to get a lot worse.

11

G arrick only became aware that Derek Fraser was in the lobby when the shouting began. He had been waiting for him in the splendid Chilston Park Hotel, just outside Maidstone. The stately, red-bricked country house had put Garrick back in time to a more elegant *Jeeves & Wooster* era when he'd driven up the driveway. Fraser was clearly sparing no expense for his temporary accommodation, and Garrick suspected his nasty solicitor was planning to bill the police for the extravagance.

He had been engrossed in his phone, so hadn't noticed Fraser skulk past on his way to the dining room. But somebody else had. There was a flash of scarlet, and a woman intercepted her prey.

"You son of a bitch!" she screamed. "Why are you still alive?"

He instantly recognised Fraser's ex-wife, Rebecca Ellis. In person, she was even more impressive. Wearing a tight black top that emphasised her bosom, and skinny jeans, she sported a healthy tan and looked more radiant than the photograph gave her credit for. Her outfit was finished off with a long bright scarlet long coat that matched her lipstick.

Fraser was horrified to see her. "Becs? What're you doing here?"

"I had to see it with my own eyes! My solicitor said you'd cut me from your will! We had an agreement!"

"Of course I bloody cut you out! You've already bled me dry in life, so you're not getting a penny outta me when I pop me clogs!"

"You're so spiteful you even came back from the dead to rub it in!"

Garrick considered intervening as a crowd formed at a discreet distance. In the dining room, heads were turning. The staff behind the desk exchanged nervous glances. Garrick decided it was a personal moment between them, so linked his fingers together and sat back to enjoy the show.

"And I'd do it again!" Fraser screamed back.

"I'm going to make you wish you'd stayed dead."

"I wish that every time I see you, you harpy!"

Her voice dropped to a sibilant hiss. "I want it all, Derek. *Everything.*" With that, she spun around and marched from the lobby.

Fraser glanced around, his face red with embarrassment. It was then he saw Garrick walking towards him with his hands in his pockets.

"I see you and your ex still get on."

"What d'you want?"

"I wanted to ask you a few questions." He tilted his head in Rebecca's direction. "But I think I've just found somebody much more interesting to chat to. See you later."

Garrick hurried after Rebecca.

"I want to get back to me house!" Fraser roared after him.

"I don't want to be cooped up in this sty much longer!"

A five-star luxury sty, Garrick thought as he followed Rebecca across the drive to her parked hire car.

"Miss Ellis. DCI Garrick," she didn't look at his ID card, but her eyes flickered in recognition. "May I have a word?"

"I saw you on television. Some detective you are if you can't even ensure my ex-husband is dead."

"You came all the way over from Portugal just to shout at him?"

"I came because he's trying to screw me out of what is mine."

"I thought everything had been decided in the divorce."

"Not everything. Some things were best left aside. The house, for instance. To move things along, we had agreed that I get it if he dies before me, he gets the villa if I croak before him. I thought it was an amicable agreement. That way we could both hope the other would die soon."

"It must be disappointing to think you were getting a nice house, then he spoils it all by not dying."

Rebecca's smile didn't reach her eyes. There was no hint of sorrow there. "You understand my position."

"But surely his remaining assets should go to his son?"

Rebecca's eyes narrowed. "The boy isn't even his. He's as much a failure in the bedroom as he is elsewhere in life."

"But he was the reason for your divorce. The paternity test–"

"The test showed nothing. We divorced because of the affair. Plain and simple."

Garrick nodded sympathetically. "I understand. Do you mean *his* affair, or *yours*?"

A perfect eyebrow rose questioningly.

"Oscar Benjamin. The very man we are looking for. You

have been living with him in Portugal. Mr Fraser cites him as the cause for your divorce."

"Derek claims many things, doesn't he? As for where Oscar is, I would like to know that for myself. I haven't seen him since he came over here three weeks ago on business."

"What business is that?"

"His own."

"When did you last hear from him?"

She thought for a moment. "Perhaps two weeks ago. When he travels, we don't often talk. That's not uncommon when he's busy."

Garrick looked at the Hertz hire car. A small white Fiat Panda City Life. "How long are you planning to stay?"

"Not long. A short as possible."

"And if we need to contact you?"

"You can call the same mobile you people used when I was home. Not that I can imagine we'll have much to say to one another."

She opened the car to indicate the impromptu interview was over.

"One last thing, Miss Ellis. Is there anybody who would have a grudge against your husband?"

She laughed. "That is a long list. It would no doubt include you, too. You've met him. What do you think?"

She slammed the door closed and drove quickly away. Garrick turned back to the hotel and saw Fraser standing inside the doorway.

No MATTER how he angled his head, David Garrick was bewildered by the combination of shapes and colours on the painting. Any artistry or deeper meaning was so well hidden that he couldn't see it. He'd thought that he'd been too harsh in his initial opinion about Hoy's work, as people were obviously keen to throw money at it, but now looking at the two framed pieces on the wall, he was more convinced than ever that the artist must be a child.

"Not everyone gets good art," Fraser growled as he took them down from his living room wall.

Garrick was attempting to bring Fraser onside by being magnanimous and allowing him to visit his home to retrieve a change of clothes, and to gather the few personal items he required. He warned Fraser that it was still a crime scene, so he'd have to catalogue everything in and out. The first thing Fraser had done was to take the two valuable pieces of art from the wall.

"I just can't see it," Garrick admitted. "I suppose it's a question of taste."

Fraser held up one picture, alive with purple and green diagonal lines, and peppered with random yellow flecks.

"It's a question of emotion," he corrected Garrick. "Art isn't about what's easy on the eyes, it's about how it stirs you. If this doesn't elicit joy when you look it at, the taste of a Tuscan summer, the maybe you're dead inside."

Garrick couldn't rule that out. He watched Fraser carefully place the paintings in a large battered brown leather carry case. These works were twice the size of the previous Hoys sold.

"Why have you been holding these back from the market?"

"It's all about timing, detective. You build people's expectations, then let them simmer. When these go on the market, can you imagine the response?" He chuckled greedily.

Garrick looked around. The smashed patio window had

been boarded up with a plywood sheet and the glass shards removed. The bloodstain on the carpet remained as vivid as the last time he'd seen it. "I imagine it may motivate somebody else to try and kill you." That wiped the smile off the man's face. "And it's my job to see that doesn't happen," he added, remembering that he was trying to win him over. "So, talk me through the day you left here."

"It was a normal day. Raining. Had some calls. I asked Mark, at the gallery, if there'd been any interest in the two pieces down there. There was, but nobody was biting. I thought he'd pushed the price way to high."

"The last one sold for thirty thousand."

Fraser bobbed his head, unimpressed. "Right. But maybe that was a fluke? We'd expected them to fly off the wall. We got a ton of interest but..." he shrugged.

"Then they sold for a fortune after you died."

Fraser chuckled. "That's good PR for you." He became quiet as he recollected. "Then I headed off to the retreat. Got the train."

Through the doorway to the hall, Garrick noticed a keypad on the wall. "Did you put the alarm on?"

"Yes, I think so. I usually do."

"But it hadn't gone off. Who else has the code?"

Fraser shrugged. "I haven't changed it. Rebecca knows it. And anybody she told." He moved quickly to a fruit bowl and retrieved his car keys. "Looks like the moron left all the valuable stuff."

"Why did you leave your car and take the train?"

"Because it was supposed to be a relaxing break. Time for me to re-evaluate my life and plan. I can think on a train." He gestured to the paintings. "I was wondering if the art would finally come together. This was a real chance to turn my life around and get the success that was always being torn from my grasp."

"By who?"

Fraser gave a sharp intake of breath. "Women usually." He looked at the blood on the floor and became thoughtful. "Do you want my theory on who did this?"

"I'd welcome it."

"Rebecca."

"She wasn't in the country."

"No, but her boyfriend was."

"Ah, yes. Oscar Benjamin. You both had history. And he is our primary suspect."

"Becs is a conniving bitch, and I wouldn't put anything past her. She would've hated seeing me be successful, and I was getting attention with Hoy. I wouldn't put it past either of them to set up some dodgy deal on the side. They got somebody who looks a bit like me to pose for a buyer, in me own house, for authenticity. Probably trying to rip him off. It all goes wrong."

Garrick hated to admit that he was working on a similar assumption, but the paintings at Fraser's feet were a problem.

"If that was the case, why didn't they take the paintings?"

"Because if they surfaced anywhere else, questions would be instantly raised, wouldn't they? I'm the only one who knows Hoy's identity. So where would they come from apart from the dead man's house?"

"Good point."

"I do sometimes make them. If these ended up being the last two left and were stashed in some vault somewhere, then they're effectively worthless. If nobody knows they exist, then they have no value."

"Why would your ex-wife go to all that trouble?"

"I told you, because she's a spiteful cow."

"I'm not sure that would hold up in a court of law, Mr Fraser."

They went upstairs so Fraser could select clean clothes, underwear, socks, several shirts, and another suit. Garrick made a note of every item Fraser had taken, but he didn't act furtively or suspiciously. He even asked Garrick which of the two seemingly identical Hugo Boss shirts he thought looked best. With every passing minute, Fraser was becoming friendlier and more at ease.

"I'd like to speak with Hoy," Garrick said as Fraser neatly folded his clothes into a small plastic wheeled cabin bag.

"Would you now? He's not exactly a witness, is he?"

Garrick mentally noted the masculine tag. At least that ruled out half the population.

"If his work proves to be central to the case, then he may have useful information."

Fraser smiled. "I'll put in your request, Detective. You gotta remember, everybody wants to speak to him. His whole brand is based around anonymity."

"How did you meet?"

Fraser slowed his packing and ruminated thoughtfully. "It was at a small art fair. Brighton, I think. I thought the pieces had promise, so I asked if I could represent him. I'll be honest, I had no idea what I was supposed to do. I had this vague idea about creating this enigmatic figure."

"A Banksy. Wasn't that Terri Cordy's idea?"

"No, it weren't!" he snapped angrily. He roughly closed the case and zipped it up. He breathed sharply in, then calmed. "She had some smart ideas about marketing, but the Banksy thing was my idea."

"Why did you break-up?"

"Why d'you think?" Garrick shrugged, encouraging him to continue. "Because she started insisting that kid was mine."

"But you didn't leave her when you first found out."

"Well, no. I had hoped that maybe it was mine. But then I realised she was just after me money."

"And it led to your divorce."

"Becs was cheating on me too. Our marriage had died years ago."

He lifted the case and headed downstairs. In the hallway, Fraser selected a pair of tan deck shoes and put them in his case. He left pairs of green wellies, blue trainers, and polished black brogues.

"You have to admit all of this hasn't done your reputation any harm."

Fraser grinned. "No. It's the best thing Becs has ever done for me. Aside from the divorce."

"You're convinced it's her?"

Fraser took the lather carry case containing the paintings. "She's got everything to gain. You heard how mental she was about not getting the house. Made her come all the way over here." He chuckled. He opened the front door and gestured for Garrick to step outside first.

Garrick took in the front of the house, which looked quite beautiful in the spring daylight, despite the SOCO tent still attached to the wing. Garrick took the door keys and locked up.

"Nice place. How much is it worth?"

"About one-point-four million."

Garrick whistled appreciatively. "And who would benefit from it? Who's your next of kin?"

Fraser smirked and walked to the garage. "I don't like

anybody but me benefiting. I've been trod on all my life."

He opened the garage, revealing the black Mercedes inside.

"I can see how you've suffered," Garrick said under his breath.

Fraser carefully laid the painting bag and suitcase in the boot.

"How long are you planning to stay in Chilston Park?"

"Until you let me back here. Besides, I won't be going too far now I know Becs is around. You need to keep an eye on her, Detective. I feel unsafe."

Garrick watched gravel spray as the Mercedes sped away. Fraser had confirmed his own suspicions about Rebecca Ellis. The team had put together an extensive background check on her. She had trained to be a nurse but dropped out before graduation to travel the world with her boyfriend at the time. She returned alone as that relationship fell apart. Since then, she appeared to have sofa-surfed, and lived off the proceeds of a handcrafted jewellery website she ran. It turned over just enough to pay the bills. She only found her feet when she met Derek Fraser. They'd been married for six years, during which it looked like she had spent a lot of his money, before ending up living just south of Lisbon with Oscar Benjamin. If she was working with Oscar Benjamin on anything illegal, why would she jeopardise everything by coming over?

His phone buzzed. It was a message from Drury demanding another update by the end of the day. He noticed a dozen emails from various reporters and a missed call from Molly Meyers. He wondered how she had found his number.

There was a text from Wendy with a few more details about their date. Well, that was some good news at least.

12

The evidence board was looking unusually sparse. Derek Fraser's picture had been moved to the side, with the victim now in the centre. Social media images of Oscar Benjamin, Terri Cordy, Rebecca Ellis and Mark Kline-Watson had been placed prominently down the side. DC Fanta Liu had used a picture of Hoy's artwork to represent the mysterious artist.

The team sat quietly as Chib finished the update. Uncharacteristically, Superintendent Margery Drury had not interrupted. Garrick waited for her to unleash hell about the lack of progress, especially as media speculation was rising.

"That's all we have?" she said quietly. "Plenty of motivations to discredit Mr Fraser, but without a valid ID on the deceased, we can't conjure up any motives."

"That's where we're up to, ma'am," said Garrick, swapping places with Chib in front of the board. If anybody was going to take the verbal assault, it was his duty. "At this moment we're increasing efforts to track down Oscar Benjamin. We're talking to Border Force and liaising with the police in Lisbon.

None of his associates want to talk openly about him, but they're all happy to bad mouth Fraser. When he lived here, Oscar used to make regular visits to his brother, Noel. But he's only made one since he arrived back. And that was a fortnight ago."

"He's gone to ground."

"We had an interesting comment," said Sean Wilkes, speaking up for the first time. Drury's unblinking gaze caused him to stop talking.

"Speak up, Sean," prompted Garrick.

Wilkes cleared his throat. "I was told that Oscar had been boasting about a big score coming up and he was looking for people. But everybody agrees he avoids doing anything illegal himself. He'd even sacrificed his brother to stay clean. That's why he's never been arrested. People don't want to work with him no more, but everybody is too afraid to speak out."

"Still, that sounds promising." Drury removed her glasses to rub her tired eyes. "The storm is still rumbling, and until we have something solid, I don't want anybody speaking to the press."

"Suits me fine," said Garrick.

"But in the meantime, Mr Fraser is milking every opportunity. I hear he's even had an invitation onto the Graham Norton show."

"Wow, I wonder if he can get me an autograph," Fanta said, instantly regretting it. She spoke quickly, hoping to defuse Drury's anger. "Um, it also seems Mark K-W, uh, Kline-Watson has become something of a name too. Well, within the art world, if that counts."

Drury nodded. "Now he has a lot to gain from all of this too."

Fanta looked doubtful. "I had a good talk with him. He seemed nice, and it looks like him and Fraser both got on. Mark was telling me he'd always fancied himself as a pilot. It turns out Fraser had been taking a few lessons in a private strip at Bridle Farm. They'd even discussed doing lessons together when the owners get back from their second home."

Drury nodded thoughtfully. "Regular rich boys' club."

"Mark definitely sees Hoy as a turning point in his career."

"Could he be trying to blackmail Mr Fraser?"

"I don't know how. He told me he'd paid Fraser what he owed him and seemed very happy with his commission."

Garrick looked up. "I thought we'd told him not to make that transaction?"

"Since Fraser was alive, he couldn't think of a good reason not to pay him." Garrick harrumphed, but didn't have a good comeback. "And he is very excited about the two more pieces of work that are coming through. Like I said, he thinks they're going to be game changers."

"I've seen them," mutter Garrick. "They're game changers alright. Testing how much suckers will pay for crap."

"This is feeling more like an extortion case with every passing minute," Drury mused.

Chib tapped Mark's picture. "If he had direct access to Hoy, then he wouldn't need Fraser, and that'd increase his profit margin. He already takes thirty per cent. Fraser takes twenty. That's a lot of money."

"Speaking of money," said Garrick, sitting on the corner of a desk as he studied the board. "Fraser's ex-wife stands to gain one-point-four million *if* she gets the house."

"I thought you said she wasn't in the will?" said Drury.

"Well, no, but she didn't know that before the murder."

"Who gets the house?" asked Chib.

"He wouldn't say. And we can hardly demand he turns over his own will as evidence into the death of a stranger. Even so, *before* Rebecca Willis was aware of that, she thought she stood to gain a lot."

"Let's put her to the side," Chib said thoughtfully. "She was out of the country–"

"But not her boyfriend."

"True, but the only one who has anything to potentially gain by impersonating Fraser, is the gallery owner."

"Fraser and Hoy have met. So, the only reason to impersonate Fraser was if it was to somebody outside of that circle. Maybe somebody who was representing Hoy and threatening Fraser."

"For what reason?" said Drury.

Garrick shrugged. "Maybe to demand that Fraser took a smaller commission?"

"It could be somebody who wants to represent Hoy and was threatening Fraser," Fanta suggested. "Aren't agents supposed to be ruthless?"

"But killing to get a client seems harsh," said Harry Lord.

Everybody fell silent as they contemplated this. DC Fanta Liu shifted with embarrassment.

"That's not bad, Liu," Drury finally said. "They could have brought in some hired muscle to put pressure on him, and it all went wrong."

"That would imply Fraser knew he was about to be blackmailed, and so far, he hasn't indicated that was the case, or that he'd hired a lookalike. He kept telling me he's afraid of Rebecca. And that brings us back to Oscar."

"Since Oscar Benjamin and Fraser know each other, it

stands to reason Oscar would hire other people to do the thug work."

"The big score..." mused Wilkes.

Chib nodded. "And maybe that's why nobody recognised the double?"

Garrick paced, a habit he always found helped him unravel problems. He was literally walking through the various strands. "Which again suggests Fraser planned the lookalike. Why wouldn't he tell us about that?"

"If he admits that, he may risk losing Hoy to this rival," said Chib.

Garrick was an old enough hand to know that cases shifted like sand. Half the skill of being a good copper was an active imagination. There was no point in blindly following the clues as they led over the horizon. Active, solid detection was all about thinking ahead and finding a way in front of the villain's path; not running to catch up. Everything that had been mooted this evening sounded hollow and thin. Still, the meandering line of enquiry seemed to satisfy Drury. She stood and headed for the door.

"I would like a set of bullet points five o'clock each day, marking where we are on this. And remember, nobody is to talk to the press. A polite, no comment, this is an ongoing enquiry, is more than enough." She nodded to herself, as if that answered an unspoken question. "Night everyone."

After an unenthusiastic chorus of *"Night, ma'am,"* everybody swapped relieved looks.

"I thought we were in for some verbal there," said Harry Lord, huffing out a pent-up breath.

"I think DC Liu's quick-thinking may have bought us more time," said Chib.

Fanta gave a mock bow in her seat. "You're all welcome."

The beginnings of a new migraine were revealing themselves to Garrick. The rest of the team were logging off computers and reaching for their coats as he stared intently at the evidence wall, willing it to offer answers.

"We should put some surveillance on mister double-barrel," he said, looking at an image of Mark Kline-Watson.

Chib was fastening up her coat. "A request for a full surveillance team won't happen overnight."

"Then we'll do it. Harry?"

He didn't need to turn to see Harry Lord's look of disappointment. "Um, sure, sir."

"I'll help," volunteered Fanta eagerly. She wasn't shy about her desire to get out beyond the desk, which put Garrick in an awkward position, as she was much more useful in the incident room. He threw a cautious look at Harry Lord and nodded. Fanta punched the air with a barely audible, *"yes!"*

THURSDAY PASSED SLOWLY. Lacking the resources to watch the gallery twenty-four hours a day, DC Harry Lord devised a rota that would take him, Liu and Wilkes in eight-hours shifts, from the morning until near midnight. As Mark lived above the gallery, and only left for coffee and lunch, it turned surveillance into tedium. By the end of her first shift, Fanta was already grousing about how dull their target was. The only thing of note they had to report was that the two new Hoys hanging in the gallery were attracting a constant stream of visitors, including reporters. That seemed to make Mark Kline-Watson increasingly happy. Every time they saw him through the wide gallery windows, he was on his phone.

Garrick received word that Fraser was heading into

London to recount his amazing 'back from the dead' story on the Graham Norton show, which would be broadcast the following evening. He was thankful that he would be out of the house and, he could hardly bring himself to acknowledge this, *watching a musical*, rather than see the Scotsman pontificating on national television.

Chib trawled through the divorce records between Fraser and Rebecca. She called the solicitors on both sides and was surprised to hear them say that the proceedings had been amicable. The only bone of contention had been the property, but it was Rebecca who suggested that the surviving party should inherit the other's home. With no children, it had seemed a sensible solution.

Reading through the case notes, one fact puzzled Garrick. Fraser had booked the retreat in Hay under a false name: Ben Thornley. It was a discrepancy that nagged him until he picked up the phone and called Fraser, who was on the high-speed train to St Pancras.

"I'm not going to use me real name at an art retreat, am I?" said Fraser in a voice so low, Garrick had to turn his phone's volume up. "They're a bunch of wannabe artists, and if they got wind that there was a famous dealer amongst them, it'd hardly be a quiet getaway for me, would it?"

They were cut off as the train entered a tunnel, but the excuse was in line with Fraser's ego. Garrick couldn't imagine people would consider him famous, but then again, people were always looking to network.

That made him think back to Terri. She had studied art and had kindled Fraser's own passion in the subject. Would she have tried to use his increasing fame in the art world to get her own foot on the ladder? But if her child wasn't Fraser's son, and the paternity test had proven that, what did he owe her? He couldn't think of anything she could use to blackmail him.

By three o'clock, Garrick felt an unexpected wave of nausea hit him. He hadn't slept very well for the last few nights and had been feeling a little lightheaded in the morning. He had put that down to stress, but now as he clutched the sink in the station washroom, he felt the room spin. Hunching over the sink, he splashed cold water on his face.

The thump of a cubicle door closing made him look sharply up. He was certain nobody had entered. He'd been concerned about anybody finding him looking like a junkie going cold turkey. The room was no longer spinning, but there were still the vestiges of motion with a slight drift to the left, which would suddenly reset and then repeat.

The cubicle door clanged again. It hadn't been locked, as if somebody was holding it from behind. Curious, Garrick walked over. Somebody was in there. Through the gap between the floor and door he could see shadows move and hear the shuffle of shoes.

"Hello?" No answer. "Are you alright in there?"

The absence of any reply was unusual. This was a police station, not public washroom. If this was one of the lads trying to wind him up, then they would suddenly find themselves at the end of a temper he often kept hidden.

He pushed the door open. The cubicle was empty.

Garrick took a breath. The gentle swaying stopped. He pulled to door closed and checked the shadows. There were none.

"Shit..." he mumbled. Then took out his phone and made an urgent call.

.   .   .

HE WANTED to squint against the bright light, but Dr Rajasekar prised an eyelid open.

"Look straight ahead," she said, so close that he could feel her breath on his ear.

After a moment, she turned the light off and sat back behind her desk to type her notes on the computer.

"Your pupils are fine. Although I wish you hadn't driven over here. Next time, get somebody to give you a lift," she admonished.

Rajasekar was the consultant looking after the *lump* in his head. She had mentioned hallucinatory side effects could be an issue if the tumour grew and pushed against his brain. He had called her straight away to book an emergency appointment and then driven to Tunbridge Wells.

"Your blood pressure is elevated too. I put that down to stress. Let's monitor it. You are sure you haven't had any episodes like this before?"

Garrick shook his head, although he was wondering if that was true. He was sure his recollection was a bit off, and after receiving a phone call he had thought was from his sister – his dead sister – he was feeling uneasy. Such comments appearing on his medical file would mark the end of his career.

"I am going to book you in for another MRI, although it may take a while to get an appointment."

"You think it's..." he pointed to his head.

"Let's not leap to conclusions. That's why I want another MRI. My instinct is telling me this is a combination of medication, stress, and a chronic lack of sleep. I'm going to prescribe you something to ensure you get some rest."

Garrick rolled down his shirt sleeve. His arm was still

tingling from the four successive blood pressure tests the doctor had given him.

"I'd rather avoid sleeping tablets."

"It may be a choice between them, or hallucinations brought on by fatigue. What do you prefer?"

What choice did he have?

Rajasekar sent the prescription off to print, then steepled her fingers under her chin as she watched him put his Barbour on.

"I am aware of how worrying something like this can be, David. Not just for the physical implications, but also career ones."

Garrick didn't meet her gaze. It was as if she could read his mind.

"But it is important that you and I have an honest relationship. I am under no obligation to your employers, that is your responsibility."

"I know."

"So please tell me if you have any reoccurrences. Any slight doubt that you are experiencing issues. It's purely between you and me. Your health is the most important thing."

Garrick forced a smile. "I assure you, doctor. You will be the first to know when I start to see my victims rise from the grave."

Rajasekar gave a gentle laugh. "Lucky for you, we all saw that on television. That was not a hallucination"

Garrick's smile faltered. For a moment he'd blissfully forgotten that Fraser's reappearance had been broadcast live on international television.

"Okay. Perhaps that was a bad example."

Despite his reluctance to use sleeping pills, he headed up

the hill to the Boots pharmacy in Royal Victoria Place to get the prescription. The pharmacist quickly processed the order and, stopping at Greggs to buy two sausage rolls, he was halfway down York Road, heading for his parked car, when a voice from behind startled him.

"David!" DCI Oliver Kane was jogging the last few steps to catch him up. "I thought it was you."

Garrick glanced around suspiciously. The road was mostly residential, and he was yards away from the main Mount Pleasant thoroughfare.

"Yeah. Fancy bumping into you. Sorry I can't really stop and chat. I have to be somewhere."

"Me too. I'll walk with you."

Garrick's mind was jumping from the rational to irrational in just a few short hops. Was Kane following him? Had he seen him enter his Consultant's office, or even buy his prescription? Not that it should matter... but the timing felt wrong.

"I see your Mr Fraser is enjoying the limelight."

"He may be a bit brusque, but if I was in his shoes, I'd probably be doing the same."

"Would you?"

Garrick ignored the hanging question. He quickened his pace, forcing Kane to huff for breath as he spoke.

"I'd hate to be caught up in something like that. Everybody watching your every move. The pressure to crack the case must be horrendous."

The media had made and destroyed good police reputations in their pursuit for a neatly packaged story. And it wasn't only the press or public who wore people down. He had known good officers fall into depression as their colleagues jibed them just for being at the centre of a high-profile investigation. God help the ones who had been at the epicentre of a collapsing case. Their careers had essentially stopped there and then. But those perils happened to other people. It wouldn't happen to David Garrick. Of that, he was sure. He'd admit to many flaws, but lack of determination was not one of them.

"So, this is where John Howard's lockup is." If Kane was playing games with him, he might as well do the same.

"Wish I could tell you, David. Really do. I think your input in the wider life of your friend would be most useful, but you know how it is. Somebody would point out your personal connection and that could compromise evidence."

Garrick silently noted the two direct references to how close he and John Howard had been. He doubted that was coincidental. It was exactly the type of provocation he would use against a suspect.

"I can't imagine you're here just to stalk me," Garrick gave a fake laugh.

Kane laughed too. "I was wondering if you ever picked up any parcels for Howard?"

"Not that I can think of. Why?"

"He sourced books from all over the world and used a variety of couriers. In addition, he was pushing his more macabre items for sale on the web, so..."

"I suppose the best way to ship a lamp with a shade made from human skin would be to use a reputable courier. FedEx, DHL, somebody you can rely on to get it to your customer unopened and in one piece. But I wouldn't want to tell you how to do your job."

"I was just asking."

"Most of my time with John was spent in his bookshop. I can count a handful of times over the years that we met else-

where, which I have told you already. He never came to my
house. Never came to my place of work." Garrick shrugged,
there was nothing more to say.

"Did he know where you live?"

"Maybe. We didn't send each other Christmas cards. He
never came to my house or had anything delivered. I would
always pick up books in person." They reached Garrick's car.
"This is me. Can I give you a lift anywhere?" It was a disin-
genuous question, so he was relieved when Kane shook his
head.

"No, thank you. I have a lot to do here."

Garrick hoped that Kane's gesture toward his consultant's
office was just coincidental. Not that his doctor would give
away the slightest information, not even an admission that he
was a client. Not without a search warrant. And what would
Kane need one of those for?

Garrick was suddenly struck by how paranoid he was
sounding. Was that another side effect he should look out
for? He couldn't remember.

He sat in his car and caught his breath. The encounter
with Kane had rattled him more than he'd like to admit. He
appreciated that a nuanced investigation into John Howard
was required, and his own affiliation, not only as an old
friend, but being instrumental in his death, had to be scruti-
nised. He just couldn't fathom why Kane was being so
circuitous with his questions as he clumsily tried to tease
some specific information.

He turned the engine over on the second attempt, and
once again thought about getting a new car. Or at least, a
slightly less elderly one. He turned the heater on full to clear
the fogged windscreen. As the asthmatic wheeze came
through, he scrolled through his emails. Amongst them was

one from DC Fanta Liu. Nearing the end of an uneventful shift, she reported a woman entering the gallery and arguing with Mark Kline-Watson. She had attached several pictures taken from her phone's camera.

The body language was aggressive on both sides, and the meek-looking Kline-Watson was treating her to a black look. He couldn't make out her face, but the woman was no pushover, and in several photos, she was coiled to strike. The last two pictures showed her storming from the gallery and returning to her car.

A white Fiat Panda City Life.

There was no mistaking Rebecca Ellis's distinctive red coat, trailing like a savage scar against the gallery's white brickwork.

13

"You looked dishy on TV."

Garrick rolled his eyes, his cheeks hurting from the rictus of self-pity he'd been pulling since he sat down with Wendy.

"You mean, when I was completely thrown and looked terribly confused as I made an arse of myself on national television."

"International. They played the clip on the James Corden show."

"Wonderful."

Wendy smiled and reached across the table to squeeze his arm. "I'm teasing. But until that moment, you came over very authoritative. And you look good in a suit."

"It's turning out to be an unusual case. The very type that makes you fantasise what early retirement will look like."

"Now *that's* exciting."

Drizzle ran down the window of the Canterbury Tales pub, affording them a view across the road to the Marlowe Theatre where people were slowly gravitating for the evening show. Garrick was in no hurry; he was enjoying talking to Wendy. After a sluggish Friday at work, she was a welcome relief, making him smile when he didn't feel like it. She unconsciously pulled goofy faces as she imitated people when recounting incidents at work, it was a look that he was finding adorable. And that was worrying him.

They had little in common, but Garrick suspected that was down to him not having many interests outside of crime, yet they were never stuck for conversation. It may meander and be unfocused, but it felt natural.

"I always saw retirement as a long way off," she said, sipping her house white wine.

"To be honest, I'd never considered it before." He rolled the stem of his wine glass between his thumb and forefinger, watching the liquid swirl back and forth. "When my sister died, all I wanted to do was get back to work." Her long silence caused him to look up at her. Wendy was watching him sympathetically. She'd dropped a few probing questions on previous dates, but he'd never risen to the bait. For a fleeting moment he felt like unloading his inner torment but looking at her, and anticipating an evening ahead of mindless entertainment, he decided not to bring the tone down. He forced a smile. "That makes me sound as boring as my fossil collection."

She laughed. "And when do I get to see this infamous collection?"

"Oh, you'll be disappointed. It's very much in single figures," he chuckled, before realising he had missed the possible hidden-meaning. Intrigued, he glanced up at her. She was now looking at the theatre as more people arrived. The moment, if there really had been one, had gone.

"Tell me what life was like this time last year." Wendy

swirled her glass and peered at him from over the rim. Overtly personal questions were something they'd both tactfully stepped around. Garrick sensed this one was more pointed than usual.

"Very similar." His oblique answer failed to get a reaction.

"How has a man like you reached such a wise old age without attempting it? Marriage, I mean."

"Oh. I'm not that old..."

"41. It's on your *Heartfelt* profile."

Garrick wondered if putting his age on the dating app had been a good idea. "Well, when you put it like that..."

"Are we talking a deep tragedy here? Just so we can avoid it. After all, you are the strong brooding type."

"I am?"

"Clearly." She sipped her drink and peered into the middle-distance. "Or are there children in some far-flung city that you've never got to know because you're married to your job?" She gave a playful smile, but her words were serious. "Were they a series of ships passing in the night, or are we talking about hitting a few icebergs here?"

"I've had two long relationships, both without children, both without incident." He hated himself for such a placid confession; especially as it wasn't completely true. "I suppose I never made the steps to make the relationships anything more interesting, and as a result they just fizzled out."

"Fizzled?"

He tried to convince himself that she was satisfied with the answer. "What about your dark history?"

She laughed. "Oh, icebergs the entire way!" They both laughed. She took another sip, then put down her glass and smiled. "So how much do you think you'll hate the show tonight? On a scale of one to ten?"

He held up both hands defensively. "Whoa. I could love it."

"It's about a bumbling detective who sings."

"And how do you know I don't sing when I'm on a case?"

She feigned a look of injury. "Ow! Haven't your poor victims suffered enough?"

"I can hold a note."

"Really?"

"Really."

"Karaoke style?" She must have seen the colour drain from his face because she burst out laughing again; a long genuine snort, which she became self-conscious of but couldn't stop. "Sorry. So sorry, but the horror on your face..."

"I have to draw some lines in the sand."

"Well, now I know." She giggled, then shifted in her seat. "I had an idea." Garrick just gave a little *uh-huh* under his breath, not wanting to see what other punishment she was planning to mete out. "I'm going on a ramble this Sunday. An organised group of about twelve of us across the Downs. I just wondered..."

"Exercise?" gasped Garrick.

Wendy shrugged. "I mean, either that or karaoke."

He watched the mischief twinkle in her eyes. The corner of her mouth was resisting a playful smile. She cocked her head, demanding an answer.

"Or am I to take it that that you lofty television celebs don't mingle with us commoners?"

Garrick leaned back in his chair and sipped his wine, hoping that he was giving off an air of nonchalance, when the very idea of a ramble in the countryside appealed to him.

"Naturally." He pretended to reluctantly consider it.

"Although I suppose my presence there would lift proceedings accordingly."

She clasped both hands together in a mocking plea, accompanied by one of the worst West Country accents Garrick had heard. "That's just what I was hoping, sir. Just a little time with us working class peasants."

They both cackled over the innocent absurdity of their actions. It felt as if a wave of relief suddenly flowed through Garrick, expunging the pent-up tension and anger he'd been harbouring for months. Perhaps longer. For a moment there was a flash of unrestrained child-like behaviour, an opportunity to ignore the distractions of adult life.

Wendy finished her wine and pointedly placed the glass down. "I shall take that as a yes." She glanced at her watch. "I'm going to the bathroom to give you a last chance to bail before we go in." She cocked a finger towards the theatre.

Garrick watched her go to the back of the bar, disappearing behind a throng of noisy revellers. And just then, it didn't feel such an ordeal to go to the theatre. Not that he'd enjoy the show.

"I HEARD YOU HUMMING ALONG," accused Wendy as she put up her compact umbrella to fend off the increasing rain.

"You're hearing things," Garrick replied guiltily.

"David Garrick, you're a terrible liar." She put the umbrella up and hooked his arm, pulling him close so they could both benefit from the shelter as they walked to the multi-story car park on Station Road West.

"Okay, it wasn't as bad as I thought. That bloke from the telly was a surprisingly good singer."

"He's a comedian. Quite famous too."

"I don't watch a lot of television."

"And was the killer obvious to your police detection powers?"

"Actually no, because I'm off duty." In fact, he had been completely wrong in the rather simplistic whodunnit. He was about to comment further when he did a double take at the young Asian woman walking towards them. "Fanta?"

Fanta Liu froze mid-stride, alarm plastered across her face. She was linking the arm of Sean Wilkes, both under a sensible large red golfing umbrella.

"David... um, DCI... sir," she stuttered, immediately shucking off Wilkes's arm. He looked as if he'd seen a ghost.

"Evening, sir," Wilkes managed.

Garrick felt a sudden pressure to relieve the tension. He looked at Wendy and gestured to his two juniors.

"This is Sean Wilkes and Fanta Liu. Two of my team. Fancy seeing you here."

"Pleased to meet you," beamed Wendy, enjoying every moment of their combined awkwardness.

Fanta and Wilkes exchanged a look. "Funny, because we bumped into each other too."

"Really?" said Garrick in a tone made it clear the world knew that was a lie.

"We went to see a magician," said Wilkes, his cheeks flushing.

Fanta nodded. "He was very good." She waved one hand, then opened the other. "You really didn't know where to look." She winced under Garrick's gaze. "I didn't peg you for a musical fan, sir."

Garrick frowned and then realised that Wendy was clutching a programme from the show.

"Ordinarily, no. But me and my friend decided... why not?"

Fanta smiled. "Uh-huh. You're friends." She didn't believe him.

"Well, don't let me keep you two from enjoying the evening."

Fanta's eyes widened. "I'm going straight home. To bed. Alone," she instantly regretted saying that. She quickly added, "I'm on surveillance early."

They quickly parted with a round of goodnights. Wendy gripped Garrick's arm harder as she burst out laughing. It was then Garrick noticed he hadn't let go of her.

"They are so terrified of you! What kind of monster are you in work?"

"The very best kind."

He drove Wendy home in Lenham, and they chatted about the musical and other distractions before finally circling back on the promise to go rambling on Sunday. If she promised to go easy on him, then it was a date.

Outside her house, she kissed him gently on the lips and smiled. He looked into her dark brown eyes and suddenly wanted the night to extend a little longer.

"Goodnight, detective." Her smile broadened as she got out of the car and hurried to her door. After hunting for her keys, she opened it, gave a little wave, and disappeared inside.

Their dates had been a slow progression from the first disaster, each steadily improving. They had kissed a little, but nothing wildly passionate. There had been no hint that she wanted to jump into bed with him just yet, and Garrick was relieved by that. She was three years younger than him, and he fretted that the scars of the last few months, combined with his general lack of activity on the dating scene, had made him rusty, to say the least. He was quite content with the slow pace.

The tortured screech of the windscreen wipers jarred him from his reverie. He turned on the radio. He pulled away as some nineties love ballads crooned from Radio 2. For the first time, he was looking forward to the weekend. He marvelled that life could still be full of surprises.

14

T he excessive blood looked almost unnaturally vivid against the spotless white linoleum floor. It was like an art exhibit unto itself, even with the battered head of Mark Kline-Watson sprawled in the wide crimson pool.

Garrick looked down on him with sorrow. He may have been a suspect, but the young man certainly didn't deserve the brutal blow against his temple with a piece of his own artwork. The Mobius stone snake sculpture had been tossed aside as the assailant fled.

He stepped aside as the white-suited SOCOs moved around him. Still ashen, DC Liu stood in the corner. He crossed to her, but her gaze never left the corpse.

"Maybe you should get a drink. Let SOCO do what they need to."

Fanta shook her head. Her hands were stuffed in the pockets of her puffer jacket, but he could see they were shaking. She was wearing a biscuit-shade hoodie top underneath, blue jeans and trainers, a perfect non-uniform for surveillance.

"Alright then. Talk me through it."

Fanta cleared her throat. "I turned up at seven-fifty-three and parked over there." She indicated to a street outside. "I had a thermos, with some coffee. I poured one and sat until about five past nine. That's when I thought something was off. He opens at nine," she said by way of explanation. "And the boys," as she referred to Wilkes and Lord who were alternating shifts with her, "all kept pointing out how anal, um, precise his timekeeping was. I crossed over and peered in. And saw his shoe poking out there."

From their vantage point near the door, they could just see his legs sprawling from behind a display cabinet. From outside, it was difficult to see much more than his loafers.

"I pushed the door. It was unlocked. I came in... then called it in." She couldn't stop her voice from quivering.

Garrick tactfully stood between her and the body. She had seen corpses before, but there was something much more personal about making the discovery yourself, alone. Garrick remembered the first time it had happened to him as a young officer. It was an OAP who had fallen and died in his flat. It had taken the neighbours four days to report it, by which time the smell had become unbearable in the summer heat. That had lingered with him for a long time, and it wasn't as graphic as Mark Kline-Watson's fate. The side of his face had caved in from the blow, breaking bones and exposing gore that shouldn't be seen outside an operating theatre.

The murder had occurred some point between midnight, when Harry Lord had finished his shift, and before Fanta's arrival. Perfectly timed in the dead zone between surveillance shifts. Had the assailant known the gallery was being watched? Or had the victim suspected?

"What's your gut telling you?" He was trying to get Fanta to think rather than dwell on the body. She was also so naturally intuitive that he hoped that some part of her subconscious was piecing together clues she had so far ignored.

She sucked in a halting breath and composed herself. "He knew his attacker. There is no signed of forced entry and it didn't look like much of a scuffle. Not to me. He's lying face down, so I reckon he had his back to the killer."

Garrick noted three security cameras positioned around the gallery space, and an alarm keypad on the door behind Fanta. As far as he could tell, nothing had been taken. Sculptures sat equidistant from each other. There were no obvious spaces amongst the artwork on the walls and, most surprisingly, the two Hoys from Fraser's house were still on the wall. Fanta followed his gaze.

"They're the two new Hoys. I watched him show them off. Strange they weren't nicked. They're probably worth more than the building now."

Theft of the paintings would be an obvious motive. The fact they were still here indicated that this was a more personal vendetta.

Fanta continued. "He has a nice watch, a Tudor. That's still on him. As is his earring. And I bet that's a real diamond."

"What about upstairs?"

"I had a quick look to make sure nobody was there. But it didn't look like anybody had been through it. Something is missing though."

Garrick looked around but couldn't notice anything obvious. "Did he have a cash register?"

"A cashbox. That's still there," she pointed to a small red tin sitting amongst bubble wrap and brown paper on a shelf under a display cabinet, just out of sight from regular punters. "His phone has gone. Remember when we first came? He clung onto it as if his life depended on it. Every time I saw him, he had it in his hand. I had a quick shufty around and can't see it anywhere."

Garrick swept his gaze around the room. "The attacker comes in, expected. After midnight. They probably argue. He gets whacked over the head. Nothing is taken other than his phone. Not even the valuable paintings that've been splashed all over the press." He looked quizzically at her. "Would you agree that's odd?"

"I suppose."

Garrick moved to the broad windows. A few paintings hung there, but the space was minimalist, offering passers-by a glimpse into the gallery.

"It would've been dark. The streetlights are over there and there," he pointed to either end of the street. "They don't shine straight in. He probably would've had some lights on. Some low-key mood lighting knowing him."

Fanta thought, then shook her head. "There were no lights on when I came in. It was all ambient." She indicated the lights that were now on. "The officers on duty must have done that."

As she was in plainclothes and had left her police ID at home, it had taken some explaining to convince the uniformed officers turning up at the scene that she was undercover. It hadn't been until Garrick had turned up, that she had been allowed out of a police car.

"Then the killer turned off the lights and shut the door," Garrick said. He eyed the parade of shops up and down the street. "There must be a few security cameras along here."

"I'll get onto it."

"No. You're heading home."

"What? Why?"

"Your role as surveillance was overtime."

"That's bollocks... sir."

"No, that's a fact that Drury will be very keen on pointing out. I need your head clear and hanging around this place will not help." She opened her mouth to argue, but he ploughed on. "Tomorrow we'll need all hands to piece this together."

They exited the building. The street immediately outside had been cordoned off to prevent people from looking into the crime scene. Patrol cars with their flashing blue lights guarded either end of the street.

Garrick walked her to her car. He only got a few yards when his name was called from behind. It was Molly Meyers, wearing a green jacket with the hood up, framing her freckled face. Garrick quietly told Fanta to go, he didn't want any of his team bombarded with questions.

"Ms Meyers. News travels fast."

"All part of the service," she beamed, then nodded at the gallery. "How about an exclusive?"

"I'm not sure how exclusive this really is. The victim is Mark Kline-Watson, the gallery owner, but I'm sure you know that."

"How did he die?"

"Gruesomely. Look, Ms Meyers–"

"Molly."

"Molly. It's too early to say anything for sure."

"What was stolen?" She stared at him with a half-smile, anticipating the answer.

"As far as we can tell, nothing at this stage."

Her smile faltered, and she jerked a thumb towards the gallery, which was only now being obscured by a damp white forensic tent. "But there are a pair of Hoys in there. They're only going up in price."

Garrick shrugged. "What can I tell you?"

"So, it's not a robbery."

"It's a murder."

Molly's brow knit together. For a moment all they could hear was the rain pelting the fabric of her hood.

"Are you sure the paintings are genuine?"

Now it was Garrick's turn to hesitate. The thought hadn't occurred to him. He recovered quickly.

"It's too early to say anything." He was relieved when he saw Chib pull up in her Nissan Leaf. "Now excuse me. It looks like I will have to do some work to answer your questions."

He ducked under the police tape barrier and hurried across to DS Okon as she locked her car.

"Morning, sir. I came as soon as I heard."

"DC Liu found him. I've sent her home." He glanced across at Molly, who was taking pictures on her phone. "I want you to bring the Hoys in as evidence."

"They weren't stolen?" she sounded as surprised as everybody else.

"We need to bring Fraser in for questioning, and Rebecca Willis too."

After a few hurried calls, Derek Fraser agreed to come in

later in the afternoon, claiming he was suffering from shock after hearing the news. Rebecca Ellis was far more evasive and told Garrick that she didn't have time to waste today but could meet him in the Costa Coffee at Maidstone Services.

Evidently, a murder wasn't enough to interfere with her social life.

15

Garrick's Land Rover refused to start so he was forced to ask Chib for the loan of her car. She handed him the keys with great reluctance. Five minutes later, Garrick was easing out of Rye in her toy car, although he was rapidly reassessing his opinion of it as he enjoyed the blistering acceleration. By the time he had made the twenty-eight-mile journey to the Maidstone service station on the M20, the fancy dashboard screen alerted him to the needed to recharge. He found an empty charging bay in the car park and wasted several minutes trying to work out where to connect the lead before calling Chib to talk him through it. Leaving the vehicle charging, and deciding electric cars were far too much of a faff to be practical, he met up with Rebecca inside the service station.

Rebecca Ellis sat at a corner table in the Costa Coffee, instantly recognisable in her bright red coat. She spotted Garrick and waved him over. Unblinking, she held his gaze as he sat down. Garrick couldn't shake the image of a venomous snake poised to strike her prey.

"Sorry for not being flexible, Detective, but my time here is limited. And after all, it wasn't as if it was a formal request," she added with a thin smile.

Garrick was already annoyed by her power play attempts, and it was all he could do to proceed civilly. He certainly wasn't in the mood for subtlety.

"Mark Kline-Watson was murdered in the early hours of this morning."

Her perfectly tanned brow wrinkled slightly. "Who?"

"The owner of Cinq Arts Gallery in Rye." He watched as she sipped her coffee without betraying a flicker of recognition. "You must remember him. You were there the other day, arguing."

She calmly put the cup down and nodded thoughtfully. "I remember him. The arrogant young man working with Derek."

"Why were you there?"

She didn't answer immediately. Her eyes flicked around the service station. It was busy with travellers rushing in to use the toilets or snatching snacks for their journey ahead.

"Derek may not have been entirely forthcoming about his financial holdings. Ones that were supposed to be declared at our divorce hearing."

"Such as...?"

"Such as offshore accounts that he and Mr Kline-Watson used. Which also made me think that perhaps he, and this mysterious artist of his, were working together when we were still married. In which case that is a vested business interest left undeclared too."

"You believe you are entitled to half of his income from Hoy?"

"Bingo." She shrugged and sipped her cappuccino.

"Derek is duplicitous man, Detective. He tells you what you want to hear, unless that is the truth, of course."

"But Hoy's art has only just started selling recently. I mean, after your divorce."

"So? Perhaps I would have like to take a stake in upcoming talent?" Garrick doubted that very much. Her dark eyes peered at him from over the grande-sized cup. The bitter smell was already making his stomach churn. His doctor had warned him not to drink coffee, and now he had recently developed a penchant for herbal teas. His migraine flared up with a sudden blinding pain across his temples. Could it be triggered by a smell? Or was Rebecca Willis proving to be more stressful than he expected? He closed his eyes and rubbed his right temple, only focusing back on Rebecca as she put the cup down against the saucer with a loud clatter.

"Are you okay, Detective?"

"Yes, fine," he managed. "Just had something that's not agreeing with me."

"My ex-husband has that effect on me."

"Tell me what you and Mr Kline-Watson discussed."

"He denied having any link to Derek's off-shore account, other than paying money into it. He refused to give me the account number, so I shouted. I consider that a reasonable reaction to somebody who is trying to swindle me. To add insult to injury, he had another two paintings that Derek had given him. He was boasting about receiving ludicrous offers for them."

"Did he say how much?"

"Two-hundred thousand. Each. A Middle Eastern buyer, apparently. Well, if they have been stolen now, that would be some good news to irritate Derek." She lifted her cup in silent cheers, before taking a sip.

"They haven't been stolen."

He watched as an eyebrow raised in surprise. Was it genuine? Her reactions all seemed too controlled, too slow.

"Where were you yesterday evening?"

"I was having a drink at the Oak Tavern in Sevenoaks with an old friend."

"He can confirm this?"

"*She* can. Yes," she snapped tartly.

Garrick opened the notepad app on his phone and slid it across to her.

"I will need details to confirm that."

She treated him to a poisonous look, then typed in a name and mobile number. Garrick glanced at it.

"Maria?"

"And old friend who lives there. I was there until eleven thirty. Then I went back to my Airbnb."

"What times were you there?" He handed the phone back. "And I will need your address."

Rebecca didn't know the address by heart, so copied it from a booking email on her phone. "If I left her at eleven thirty, then I was probably there fifteen minutes later until about nine this morning when I went to McDonald's for breakfast." She reached into her coat and retrieved her purse. Sliding through a wad of carefully organised receipts, she pulled out one from the fast-food outlet and indicated to the time and date. "See?"

"Can anybody confirm you were at your lodging all night?"

"Of course not. Can anybody confirm where you were last night?" She raised a suggestive eyebrow and put the phone and purse back in her coat pocket.

"What makes you think he knew the artist when you were married?"

"Aside from the fact that he's a serial liar?" She frowned when Garrick shook his head. "You must know about his affair. She had connections in the art world. That's when his interest started up."

"It's possible that he could have started representing Hoy afterwards."

She put the cup down and leaned across the table, her voice dropping in volume. "Derek is talentless. He doesn't know one end of a paintbrush from another. When we were living together, he had no interest in art. And then suddenly, he is an expert? Please!"

She leaned back as Garrick digested this.

"And what does your boyfriend think of all this?"

She angrily snatched her cup. It was the first genuine emotion she'd displayed.

"I wish I knew. I haven't seen him if that's what you want to know. He doesn't have a house over here anymore, and what few friends he had haven't seen him either. I don't know where he is. And I'm worried."

"Why did he come over?"

"Business. I respect him, so I never pry into what that means."

"He spent most of his time with you in Portugal?"

She tilted her head coquettishly. "Do you blame him?" She sighed and waved a hand around. "After all, what's here for either of us? Terrible weather and suspicious people." She looked pointedly at him. "Oscar has done nothing wrong. His brother is doing time, not him. Yet everybody thinks he is the criminal."

Garrick gently tapped his hand on the table. "He's the one with the reputation."

"We all have reputations, don't we, Mister Garrick? You have the unfortunate reputation of bringing my ex-husband back from the dead. That's how the world regards you. I wonder how deserving is that? I'm sure you've done many good things in your life too."

"Where is he, Rebecca?"

She leaned back, her nose wrinkling. "I told you. I wish I knew. I really wish I knew." A hint of vulnerability crossed her face. "He hasn't answered his phone for over a week. Your manhunt seems to have terrified him."

Garrick leaned forward. "That surprises me. Considering how innocent you paint him. Why would a man with nothing to hide, suddenly disappear?"

Rebecca breathed heavily through her nose and glowered at him. He'd touched a nerve.

He softened his tone. "How were things between you?"

"Fine."

"You'll forgive me for saying that it doesn't sound very fine at all. In fact, it sounds like quite a tangled mess. Oscar claimed that your ex-husband owed him money. Then you both run off together. Some clarification over that would help."

Rebecca gave a dismissive gesture. "What is there to say, other than you are blowing it all out of proportion. Oscar and I fell in love. It's as simple as that. Were we bonded by a mutual loathing of Derek? Perhaps. It's always nice to have some common ground in a relationship. As for the money, you know Derek owned a scrapyard. He was struggling with cash flow. Oscar's brother was somehow involved with it too and convinced Oscar to lend him the money. He did not

MURDER IS SKIN DEEP

115

know that they were up to their necks in anything illegal. Neither did I. Derek served his time, which was a blessing because that is when Oscar and I found one another. Although we didn't start dating until much later."

"Such a romantic story," said Garrick wryly. "And how much was owed?"

"I believe it was about two-hundred grand."

"A not inconsequential amount. A tidy sum for Oscar to have down the back of the couch."

"He's a businessman. And in that instance, his judgement was clearly off." She glanced at her watch. "I'm afraid I must go. Time waits for nobody."

"What's the rush?"

"I'm returning home in a couple of days. I only came over to see for myself that Derek was still alive. Just in case it was all some horrible dream." She stood, touching her pocket to confirm her purse and phone were still there. "Like you, I am eager to find Oscar."

"And you will let me know as soon as you do."

"Of course."

"When are you leaving?"

"The twenty-eighth. A pre-booked return flight before you accuse me of fleeing the country."

"I'll need to talk to you again before you go." She cocked her head, annoyed, but she said nothing. "You need to be formally eliminated from our enquiries."

"Good luck, Detective."

Unsmiling, she hurried out, high-heeled black boots click-clacking on the smooth floor. Garrick watched her for a moment, his mind racing. Everything she had said amounted to a torrent of motivation for her to wanting to kill Derek. The problem being that he wasn't the one who had died, otherwise this may have been an open and shut case. Her reaction to Oscar's disappearance was the most genuine she'd given, but he doubted the reason she had flown over from Portugal was to just to confirm that her ex-husband was alive. There was more to it than that. She was being less than truthful.

The migraine had receded to a dull throb. He hadn't taken the sleeping pills that Dr Rajasekar had prescribed as he was still concerned about using them, but now he was regretting it. He'd hoped for a lie-in today, especially as he hadn't been able to sleep because he kept thinking about his date.

Christ, Wendy... tomorrow's rambling escapade would have to be postponed. She had been so insistent that he imagined she'd be gravely disappointed. Or he hoped she would be. At least she was experiencing the difficulties of dating a detective now rather than later. Better to end it early before anybody gets hurt, he thought despondently.

On impulse, he quickly stood and walked out of the service station. Across the car park he saw Rebecca Ellis getting into her rented Panda. He trotted to Chib's Nissan Leaf and sat inside – before remembering it was still connected to the electrical charger. By the time he got back out and unplugged the vehicle, Rebecca was following the one-way flow out of the car park.

The Nissan's electric engine started immediately, although Garrick had to check as it was utterly silent. In seconds he was speeding far too quickly in pursuit. He kept a discreet distance as they passed the petrol station and looped onto the roundabout. A delivery van inserted itself between them, offering a degree of anonymity. He followed Rebecca onto the westbound M20. He kept two cars between them as she diligently stayed to the speed limit. Garrick had assumed she was heading back to her rented accommodation and wondered about the wisdom of following her, but when she turned off onto the A228, he became intrigued. This would be a much longer route home. Soon they were on the A26 and heading to Tonbridge. He was curious to what was drawing her here.

Then a chime from the dash. A warning that he had little battery charge left.

"What?" he thumped the wheel. Why hadn't it recharged? A map appeared on-screen with the closest charging station being at a BP garage half a mile ahead. If he didn't stop there, then he would roll to a halt in minutes. Frustrated, he turned onto the petrol station forecourt and watched Rebecca's car disappear around the bend.

16

D S Chibarameze Okon had been thinking ahead with the textbook diligence Garrick was coming to expect. After taking the two Hoy paintings from the gallery to secure them in the station's evidence locker, she had contacted the London-based art expert, Jasmine Slater, who'd appeared in the Country Life article with Derek Fraser. She lived in Surrey, and the prospect of driving down to Maidstone to view the new Hoys first-hand was one she couldn't pass by.

The two pieces of artwork sat on a dust sheet to protect the frame from the floor and had been unceremoniously propped against a steel evidence rack in the small secure room at the police station. To Garrick's eye they looked just as he remembered them in Fraser's living room: awful. Jasmine Slater crouched reverently in front of each and took them in. Every so often she would sigh with delight.

"They certainly look like originals." She used her little finger to indicate the brush strokes. "See the paint is layered in the horizontal? Quite thick at times."

"Like a child slashing at the canvas," said Garrick.

Jasmine was too engrossed to pick up on his sarcasm. "Almost. Yes. The verticals are not as heavy, which is in line with the previous work. And the juxtaposition of the primary colours and primitive shapes…" Words failed her as she stood, her eyes never leaving the canvases. "The issue is that there are only a few other works to compare the artist's technique. On the other hand, that makes it more difficult for a forger because so little is known."

"But your best guess is that they're genuine?" Chib prompted.

"Indeed. Although the real expert is Mr Fraser."

"He confirmed they were real." Only thirty minutes earlier he had stood in this very room and almost wept when he saw his precious paintings were intact. "We just needed a second opinion."

Since she'd made the journey to see them, they allowed her another ten minutes of breathless appreciation, listening to her extract meaning from the abstract. They escorted her out and then made their way to the interview room.

"Since when did you become a luvvie, Chib?"

"What do you mean?"

"Nodding and gasping at all the bollocks she was touting. Were you like that in public school?"

"When an expert explains things to you, it's easier to see hidden meaning and digest it. Didn't you feel something when she explained the emotions on display? How the colours were in direct conflict with the meaning?"

"All I heard was a bunch of arty-farty bull. If art has to be explained, then it's not working. I still can't see how that junk is better than anything drawn in a nursery. Proper art should look like, whatever it's supposed to be. When I see a picture of fruit, I know what it is."

"What about the emotional trigger?"

"Yeah. I see fruit, it makes me hungry. My point is I know what I'm looking at."

Chib chewed her lip for a moment, then said, "A little girl draws a picture of a horse. Her teacher says, '*You drew the horse wrong!*' The girl looks at him and asks, '*How?*' The teacher points and says, '*You drew wings on it. It isn't a horse if it has wings!*' The little girl replies, '*Then why did you call it a horse?*'"

They stopped outside the interview room. Garrick blinked at her.

"Is that supposed to be a joke?"

"Maybe it's an allegory."

"Because jokes are also not funny if you need to explain them. That kinda proves my point."

Inside, Fraser was seated with his solicitor, Rosamund Hellberg. She had a legal pad open on the desk and had made a page of notes. She carefully closed it so Garrick couldn't see what was written.

Chib started the recording and introduced the participants. Garrick leaned on the table and looked Fraser squarely in the eyes.

"I hope you are satisfied that your artwork is safe."

"Aye, but you just better make sure you're insured too. Just in case."

"Always thinking of the important things, Mr Fraser. I commend you. After all, the paintings were the first thing you asked about when I told you Mr Kline-Watson had been murdered."

Hellberg rolled her eyes but said nothing.

Fraser pulled a face, as if the answer was obvious. "Of course. You told me he'd been murdered, so there was little point in asking if he'd gotten any better, was there? Don't mean I wasn't sorry for the lad. He'd done well selling me paintings. I couldn't fault him."

"Would you categorise your relationship as a friendly one?"

"Absolutely."

Garrick nodded. "And, because of course I have to ask, can you confirm where you were last night, between eleven and nine this morning?"

"In the hotel. Had a few snifters at the bar before going to bed. Then had breakfast there this morning. I have a question for you. He had a buyer lined up for those paintings. More than one, at least that's what he hinted at. He never told me their details. Did he leave any records, notes, emails about them? I have a duty of care to my client, you understand."

"We can look into that, but at the moment any information is held as part of a murder enquiry."

"They're my customers!" snapped Fraser. "That's my information you're withholding!"

For the first time since they'd met, Garrick saw Fraser was genuinely concerned. He understood why. The artwork was rapidly making his career, and the money offered defied common sense. As much as he disliked the man, Garrick felt sympathetic.

"I wouldn't worry. If people are willing to pay so much for them, they'll reach out directly to you."

Fraser took a sip of water as he thought about that. His expression suddenly brightened, and he nodded.

"Of course... I wasn't thinking straight."

No, thought Garrick, although now you've just realised you don't have to pay commission to the gallery either. Another death following the mysterious artist's work had all the hallmarks of more than ill fortune.

"Who did he have issues with?" said Chib.

"You mean, who'd kill him?" Fraser shook his head and thought. "Nobody I know."

Garrick and Chib swapped a look. She'd made door-to-door enquiries, and the initial response painted Mark Kline-Watson as an affable member of the community. His brief spike in popularity had a beneficial knock-on effect in the town as more visitors came to the gallery. She'd copied footage from several doorstep cameras, which DC Wilkes was currently sifting through. His own security cameras hadn't been switched on the night of the murder.

"Of course, we now really need to contact Mr Hoy."

Fraser leaned back in his seat as Rosamund Hellberg took over, opening her legal pad. Garrick suddenly had an inkling about what they had been discussing while alone.

"That is privileged commercial information."

"Hoy is a suspect."

"Really? How? He's just a name. Nobody has identified him. You don't have his fingerprints on the murder weapon. Mr Kline-Watson didn't know him or have any contact with him, and vice versa. It was all channelled through my client."

Garrick snorted in disbelief. "Are you refusing to hand over details of a person of interest?"

Fraser said nothing. He wouldn't even look at Garrick.

Hellberg smiled. "Just so we are clear, Detective. My client is not refusing any formal request whatsoever. In fact, after you publicly declared he was dead, he has been cooperating with you to the best of his ability. He has even refrained from making any legal claims against you and the force that may have damaged his professional reputation–"

Garrick couldn't hold back a derisive laugh. "Of course not! That mix-up made his name go international!"

Hellberg continued talking over him. "Instead, a man, whose identity still foxes you, was murdered in my client's house. A business associate he heavily depends on, was murdered by an assailant unknown to you. And now you insist on knowing the identity of a third person you know nothing about! Ha!" she shook her head in disbelief. "Does the phrase *chasing after the wind,* mean anything to you? Or the word, *incompetence*?"

Garrick was furious. He felt his cheeks and forehead burn, but and suspected that was because of his migraine. He was also speechless because she was partially correct.

Point firmly made, Hellberg softened her tone. "However, because he believes in helping you as much as possible, Mr Fraser will put whatever questions you have to the artist."

"That's not good enough."

Hellberg shrugged. "Just to be clear. I mean, crystal clear. Are you charging my client with anything? Anything at all?"

"No."

"And he is helping as best he can. So that is just the way things are." She closed her pad and turned to Fraser. "I think we're finished here." She stood, but Fraser made no motion to leave. His hands were now clasped together, and he wore a haunted look.

"Why do you think Mark was killed?" he asked quietly.

"We're trying to put that picture together," said Chib, flinching at her inadvertent pun.

"They didn't nick the paintings because there would be nowhere to sell them on to, really. They still have to be sold to justify their worth." Fraser was internally working through the conundrum. "And the bloke killed in my house was dressed like me. Looked a bit like me."

Garrick nodded.

"So, this is all about me." Fraser cupped both hands over his mouth. "I think they want to get to Hoy."

"Which raises the questions," Garrick held up a finger. "Who is Hoy?" Then another finger curled upwards. "Who are '*they*'?"

Fraser looked between Garrick and Chib. "I think that's obvious, isn't it? That harpy ex-wife of mine, and Oscar Benjamin. He always said he'd get his own back on me. Kept claiming I owed him money, which I don't. Blamed me for his brother being behind bars when he was a crook anyway!"

"We're still looking for Oscar Benjamin," Garrick admitted.

"Rebecca knows where he is."

"She's denying that."

Fraser sniggered. "She's a chronic liar, that woman. Why is she here? To shout at me for being alive? I haven't heard jack from her since, so it can't be that. I think they're in cahoots trying to find out who Hoy is. And if they can't do it through the people they killed, then it stands to reason they'll come after me next." He shifted nervously in his seat and looked at his solicitor. "Shouldn't I have police protection?"

Hellberg looked expectantly at Garrick. "That is a good question."

GARRICK SHUFFLED BACK into the incident room. The short time he'd spent with Fraser had drained him. He spent another twenty minutes sitting on the toilet with his eyes closed, letting the effects of two aspirin ease the pain in his head, and hopefully take the edge off the hot flush he'd experienced.

Pictures of Mark Kline-Watson's body hung on the evidence board, along with angles of the gallery taken from outside. Garrick groaned when he saw DC Fanta Liu was at her computer.

"I thought I ordered you to go home?"

"That was an order, sir? I thought it was a suggestion. I guessed that DC Wilkes could probably do with a hand going through the surveillance footage around the gallery, especially if we wanted to get it done quickly."

Garrick bit his tongue; it was no use arguing with her. Chib appeared at his side, offering a mug of tea.

"Are you okay, sir?" she asked in a low voice, filled with concern.

Garrick nodded and took the cup. "I haven't been sleeping much. And the more time I spend with Derek Fraser, the worse it is for my blood pressure."

"It's a matcha green tea." She indicated to the cup. "Might help you unwind."

He took a sip. It was exactly what he'd been craving. DS Okon's preternatural power of reading his mind had struck again.

"Harry is still at the crime scene. I think East Sussex is relieved that we're taking the lead. I don't think they want to stretch resources fighting the media. The coroner's initial cause of death is blunt-force trauma to the head. He was struck twice with the sculpture."

"That's hardly an accident. Twice to ensure he's dead."

"His phone is missing. Digital forensics are talking to the networks to see if it pings any masts. Other than that, nothing else was taken. As best we can tell. Time of death was probably between one and two. Nobody reported any banging of doors or shouting, so my guess is the visitor was expected. Harry showed Oscar Benjamin's picture around. A few people recognised him from the telly, but nobody's seen him in Rye."

Garrick moved closer to the photo of Fraser and Rebecca, grinning happily at the camera. "Other than him, she is our only suspect without an alibi."

"We haven't had a chance to checkout her Airbnb."

"I'm sure she will pluck a witness from somewhere who'll verify that she was there all night."

He sighed. Where had Rebecca Ellis been heading? It wasn't back to her accommodation, and she had left as if to keep an appointment...

"I want a sweep around Tonbridge and Tunbridge Wells. Look for Rebecca Ellis's car. Put a call out. She's not to be stopped, keep it all quiet. I just want to know where she is. Also, look at car parks. Any flags on ANPR." She was driving far too carefully to be ensnared by any traffic cameras, but with bus lanes and CCTV you just never knew your luck.

"What about protection for Fraser?"

"We can't afford an armed bodyguard following him everywhere. Besides, something just doesn't ring true. Let's assume our lookalike-theory led to our first victim. Oscar Benjamin was using some hired thugs to find out Hoy's identity. Fine. But would he repeat the same mistake at the gallery?"

"We have Rebecca Ellis there. Arguing."

"Which makes more sense if they're working together to get to Hoy..."

"Or blackmailing Fraser."

"Mmmm...."

"But why go back and kill him? And if it was a different killer, then what's the motive?"

"Perhaps Mark agreed to help? Maybe he was offered a bigger commission if they got Fraser out of the way."

"Except he claimed he didn't know Hoy's identity. Fraser confirmed that."

"Which brings it all back to Derek Fraser. They finally realise he is the sole gatekeeper. If they kill him, it would be logical to assume Hoy would turn himself over to the police instead of submitting to blackmail. Which means Fraser's on safe ground at the moment. The only option I can think of is that they would need to persuade Hoy that Fraser is a terrible agent. Poison his reputation."

"Convince him that Fraser is taking a larger cut than he should, that sort of thing?" Garrick nodded. "That's as good a theory as any. But if Fraser winds up dead in his hotel, after requesting protection, then the optics will not look very good."

"Nothing about this case is looking very good. Rebecca Ellis. That's who we need to focus on." Her arrogance irked him. She took delight in messing people around. Again, he felt an unexpected twinge of sympathy towards Fraser.

He was sure Rebecca knew where Oscar Benjamin was. They just needed to find him before the body count went any higher.

17

Yet again, DC Fanta Liu's intervention saved Garrick from a costly mistake. He'd been in the middle of texting Wendy to cancel their ramble across the Kent Downs when Fanta had passed by and glanced at his phone. An action that annoyed Garrick as he was all too aware of her acute powers of observation.

"Is that your *friend* I met last night?" she asked as innocently as possible, which was something she wasn't particularly good at. Before Garrick could snap that she should mind her own business, Fanta quickly continued. "Only it's bad form these days to let anybody down with a text message. I mean, it's one step away from ghosting. Just saying..."

She quickly walked away, fearing his grumpy wrath. She was right, of course. Garrick should have known that. It was the sort of advice his sister would've given him. Blindingly obvious advice. He called Wendy on his way home and was relieved to hear her sound sympathetic. He promised to make it up to her as soon as possible, and they had chitchatted aimlessly all the way back to his house.

On reflection, it was a welcome change. Any work-related interventions had always been met with a frosty reaction in previous relationships. He appreciated Wendy's relaxed attitude and began thinking about how he could make it up to her. Maybe another musical if she liked them so much? Perhaps *that* was a step too far...

His empty house seemed to compound his loneliness tonight. Perhaps because the day had been so hectic, or maybe it was some deeper manifestation because he wouldn't see Wendy tomorrow.

A quick meal of microwaved beans on toast raised previously unasked questions about his poor diet. He had clearly sunk into bachelorhood more firmly than he realised. He picked up his half-cleaned ammonite from the dining table and inspected it. There was a still good few hours' worth of cleaning to be done, as well as the tidying of a large chunk of matrix that he had left the fossil sitting on. Still, to his eyes, he had carved a beauty from the rock. Some of his enthusiastic air scribing had accidentally pitted the ancient shell and, in his clumsiness, he'd completely removed one of the spiralling ridges, but he prided himself that it was still recognisable. Some of the detail that he'd uncovered beneath the rock was quite breathtaking. The echoes of his migraine persisted, so any further work on it would have to wait.

He put the television on and sat on the sofa, with his feet on the coffee table. He hazarded that opening himself up to a little pop culture may give him more to talk about with Wendy. There was a few days' worth of post to go through, mostly junk that had travelled across the country, been hand-delivered through the letterbox of his house, just so he could then carry it those last few yards to the kitchen bin and its final fate in a recycling centre. A thin bank statement and an increased Council Tax bill did nothing to lift his mood. The final item was a white envelope.

Stamped from America.

Garrick didn't know anybody stateside, and he couldn't believe that Flora PD would mail him anything. Baffled, he ripped the top of the letter open with his finger. It was empty. He inserted his forefinger and thumb to widen the envelope in case he had missed something.

With shaking hands, Garrick placed the envelope on the coffee table.

Blank phone calls, the whispering voice sounding like his sister, and now this. Physical proof that somebody was trying to mess with his head. The address was written in careful block capitals using black ink. There was no legible postmark to indicate where it had been sent from. He'd ripped the top edge open, so turned the envelope around and checked the seal was firmly adhered so that nothing had fallen out. Somebody had taken time and expense to mail him an empty envelope.

A chill ran through him.

He dashed into the kitchen and found a box of plastic sandwich bags under the sink. He returned and carefully placed the envelope into one, then sealed the ziplock to make it airtight. He considered calling his contact at the Flora Police Department, who was dealing with his sister's case, but what could he tell them that would be of use? The incident had gathered headlines at the time, and America tended to have weirdos who regularly trolled high-profile cases. He decided to drop the envelope into forensics to see what they could glean from it.

His fatigue had vanished. His heart was thumping in his

chest and he felt uncomfortably hot. He opened the sleeping pills Dr Rajasekar had prescribed and took two.

"It sounds like such a nice area," said Chib, looking at the grey metal spiked fences delimiting the south Tonbridge Station carpark.

"You're thinking of Tunbridge Wells. Sorry, Royal Tunbridge Wells. Tonbridge is like the poor half-brother."

Searching through the Automatic Numberplate Recognition Cameras revealed Rebecca Ellis had parked here and bought a ticket using a dedicated app. She'd only paid for an hour, so that had ruled her out catching the train.

A line of drab terrace houses had the misfortune to overlook the car park, and the threadbare used car showroom adjacent. Garrick nodded towards it.

"Does that ring any bells?"

Chib shook her head. "Should it?"

"It used to be owned by one Derek Fraser."

Chib flashed a smile. "What a coincidence."

"Indeed. Of course, not now. Now it's owned by Stanley Matthews. An acquittance of Oscar Benjamin."

"Perhaps she wanted to know if this Matthews had seen him?"

"Let's go find out."

Cars were crammed into every available space. Even the road between the lot and the car park was used as an overspill. Most were compact Citroëns, Minis or Renaults. Sunday footfall comprised of a father and his excited son, who wore a tracksuit and baseball cap, determined to look like the sort of person who the police would pull over half an hour after the car was handed over to him.

Careful, Garrick warned himself, profiling people is a slippy slope.

Stanley Matthews was balding, overweight, and watched Garrick and Chib approach with the practised eye of somebody who could recognise the Old Bill a mile off. He was smoking a stunted roll-up as he leaned against the wall of the battered grey Portakabin he called an office. The dealership sign proudly declared: MATTY'S MOTORS.

"Mr Matthews?" said Garrick, holding up his ID card.

Matthews' bushy grey eyebrows furrowed as he glanced between the police and his potential customers.

"Uh-huh."

Garrick recognised the aura of stubbornness the man was projecting, so got straight to the point and indicated for Chib to hold up the picture of Rebecca on her phone.

"This woman came to visit you yesterday. Who is she?"

Matthews went through the motions of looking, then shook his head.

"We had a busy day yesterday. A lot of punters looking for a bargain these days."

"So I see," said Garrick, casting his eyes at the two customers. There wasn't a single space denoting a sold car. "I'm sure you'd remember a lady like her."

"I'm not a lech, ogling every bird who wants to buy a motor," Matthews snapped indignantly.

"I meant because she wore a bright red coat. Very noticeable."

"I'm colour blind."

"Look again." Matthews did and shrugged. "She parked over there," Garrick indicated to the car park. "And came straight over. We have her movements caught on the security cameras there." He nodded towards the pole-mounted CCTV cameras dotted around the car park. The only problem was their range was confined to the car park itself. A more pedantic person might have pointed out that they didn't show Rebecca Ellis entering the used car lot. From the smirk on Matthews' face, he suspected the man knew exactly what they covered.

"I see you have CCTV yourself." Garrick looked up at a pair of small security cameras on the Portakabin roof, pointing across the lot in a V-formation. "I'd like to look at yesterday's footage."

Smoke shot from Matthews' nose. "I'd be happy to oblige. If they worked. Buggers have been broken all week. Lucky for me this is a well-policed area." He grinned and nodded to the houses. "She might've gone and visited her gran. How would I know?" He saw the father wave him over; his son was excitedly pawing over a dark green Ford Fiesta. Matthews threw the cigarette down and crushed it underfoot. "'Scuse me. Got a customer." He walked away but couldn't resist turning around and tracing a finger across his stock. "Feel free to have a gander. Could do you a nice deal. They even come with the legal papers." He winked, then turned his back on them.

Chib frowned at Garrick. She hadn't had a chance to watch the footage. By the time she had arrived, Garrick had been through it with Wilkes and Fanta. "Did we see who she was talking to?"

"No. The cameras cover nothing beyond here," he said as they walked back across the adjoining road between the car park and the lot. "But she headed in his direction for sure, then came back ten minutes later. Look."

He scrolled through several videos that had been downloaded to his phone until he found the right one. He pressed play and handed it to Chib. Rebecca Ellis, wearing her distinctive coat, appeared from the direction of the dealership and marched back to her car. She was carrying a large sports holdall, and was accompanied by a shorter person, who was also lugging a similar black bag. This new addition was wearing a puffer jacket and baseball cap that obscured the face.

"Who is this?"

"No idea. But if you go to the next file…"

Chib did so and watched them stuff the bags into the back of Rebecca's rented Panda. Then they both climbed in and drove away.

"What's your instinct about this new body?"

"Could be anybody. Average build. Man or woman. Same height as Ellis."

"She is about this tall, in heels." Garrick indicated a couple of inches shorter than he was. "And it looks like the newbie is wearing trainers. Which means they're this tall." He fractionally raised his hand.

"Oscar Benjamin is taller. About my height. And really well-built." Chib walked with Garrick up Priory Road towards the busier main road. "So, it's not him."

They reached the junction and looked around. On the corner stood a large modern block of public toilets. Opposite the road was a Lidl and a bus stop; diagonally further over lay the train station. Everything was the same 1960s architecture that once held the promise of a modern vibrant town but now looked bleak and desperate.

"She left me at the service station and came straight here to pick up this person."

"Do we know where she went next?"

"Unfortunately not. Her plate didn't flag up anywhere else. We're sifting through footage from traffic cameras to see if they can spot our mystery person arriving. But I'm not holding my breath."

Garrick had slept like a log after taking the pills, but from the moment he'd awoke, he couldn't shake the fog mussing his brain. He was supposed to be leading the investigation, making insightful decisions, but instead he felt rudderless.

"Isn't she staying near Sevenoaks?" asked Chib. "That's not far. Why don't we just ask her?"

REBECCA ELLIS's Airbnb was a rather impressive new architectural build that reminded Chib of something from the TV show *Grand Designs*. With a sweeping ash and tinted glass frontage, and a grass-insulated roof, it lay at the end of a curved private driveway, just across a quiet road from Deer Park. There was no sign of the rented Panda, although Garrick noticed fresh tyre tracks in the gravel driveway. Chib found the property on her own Airbnb app.

"Two hundred quid a night," she reported. "Has its own cinema room and hot tub."

Garrick gave out a low whistle. "I thought that app was just for cheap accommodation."

"Not at all. When we got engaged, I found a castle in Scotland to stay at. It was amazing."

Garrick gave a sidelong glance at Chib. They hadn't been working together for very long, but he didn't know much about her at all.

"What's your fella's name?"

She paused for a second, as if deciding how much to say. "Michael."

That was all he was getting. "You should bring him out one night. I heard Harry was trying to organise a quiz night."

Quiz nights, like most social functions, sounded like hell to him, but he'd already decided he should make an effort with the team.

"Should I, though?"

Her scepticism made him smile. "With that attitude, you're going to end up like me."

He didn't know what to expect, but her aghast reaction wasn't it. He slowly circled to the side of the property. A solid fence protected the rear garden. It was a pricey and isolated spot.

"Thoughts, Chib?"

She was clearly thinking along the same lines. "A hotel would've been cheaper, so she doesn't want any attention or company."

"She has friends in town she didn't want to stay with. Which indicates she has something to hide. If she came back with whoever she met in Tonbridge, they were carrying enough stuff to spend more than a couple of weeks here. Contact the owners. Find out when she booked it and if she's been here before."

His mind was ticking over. Should he stretch resources and have somebody watch over Fraser? Or would it be better spent trailing Rebecca Ellis? She obviously knew more than she was letting on, and he was convinced she was protecting Oscar Benjamin... all he lacked was proof.

18

Garrick was thoughtful on the drive back to the incident room. Chib kept herself busy sending emails and making calls to track down the Airbnb owner, so she hadn't noticed. When she finally did, Garrick was rapidly shifting his gaze between the road ahead and the mirrors.

"What is it?"

"We're being followed."

It was a strange twist for Garrick. He'd followed suspects many times, but this was the first time it had happened to him. As soon as he spotted the tail, he kept his driving habits as mundane as possible, giving no hint that he was aware of their tail. He even gave a long signal as he pulled into the forecourt of the petrol station. He needed to fill up anyway, so it wasn't anything unusual. As he stopped at the pump, he watched the black Hyundai drive past without slowing.

"Are you sure?"

"Ever since we left Rebecca's place he's been behind us." Of course, it was a busy A-road back to Maidstone, and it was the most direct route. It could just be a case of paranoia, and after the last few days, that was foremost on his mind. Yet their pursuer had diligently kept two or three cars between them, no matter how much the traffic had shuffled.

He took his time filling up, paid, then pulled out of the petrol station. Three hundred yards ahead, the black Hyundai i40 Saloon was parked in a layby. With a new bout of drizzle, he couldn't make out the driver as they passed, but sure enough, the car pulled out and continued to follow him. He recited the licence plate to Chib, taking care to double-check each reversed character in his mirror. She called it in and was told it belonged to a seventy-year-old retiree from Guildford.

The car followed them all the way back to the station. As they turned into the private car park, the Hyundai continued on its way.

Garrick had an unsettling feeling he knew who was following them.

"My money is it was the press," he growled quietly. He'd received a message that Fraser had appeared on two Sunday morning shows, and a glance at the Sunday papers in the petrol station showed him that, despite the country slowly falling apart with political strife, Kline-Watson's death had made the front page.

By the end of the day, DC Fanta Liu had found more footage of Rebecca's new companion. Taken from the Tonbridge car park cameras, the newcomer could just be seen walking past the gates thirty-five minutes before Rebecca had showed up. It wasn't the clearest footage, but it had been enough for DC Harry Lord to pop into Tonbridge Station and ask to see what they had around the same time.

His hunch paid off. A fuzzy image of the figure was backtracked exiting the station a few minutes earlier. The stranger had arrived from London Bridge Station. And hadn't been carrying any luggage.

"Any guesses on what they picked up from Matthews?" Garrick asked the room.

"I'm struggling to see how this is connected to the first body or Kline-Watson," Wilkes admitted. "Rebecca wasn't in the country for the first murder."

"No. But what if she is trying to help Oscar Benjamin leave the country? If anybody knows where he is, it's her. I suspect that Derek Fraser is now too high profile a target for extortion. If that's what they were planning. And my money is on the fact Kline-Watson was in on it too. Rebecca Ellis claims she was demanding he reveal Hoy's identity. What if they were arguing because the whole thing had gone wrong?"

"And Kline-Watson was the weakest link," suggested Chib.

"So that's the link we need to expose if we are going to make any progress."

Fanta held up her hand. Garrick sighed heavily.

"I keep telling you, you don't have to do that."

"Kline-What's-His-Face was in arrears with his landlord, and I've found out he owed his bank ninety thousand in business loans he'd accrued to start the gallery, on top of previous debts. From the first Hoy sale he paid off the landlord, but his commission, even on the two new sales, wasn't enough to pay the bank who were threatening to foreclose on the business."

"Just as it was on the verge of becoming a success."

"He kept all his financial records on the computer in the gallery, but it wasn't configured for email. He must've done that on his phone."

"Which is still missing," said Chib. "We've contacted his service provider."

Fanta continued reading from her bulleted list. "All the security cameras from neighbouring premises show nothing useful. Pretty much none of them looked out onto the street."

Garrick waved an annoyed hand across the evidence wall. "Time and time again, we are facing a series of dead-ends."

"Not entirely." All eyes turned to DC Sean Wilkes, who blushed at being the sudden centre of attention. "I mean, it might be a red herring, but Tonbridge got in touch over Oscar Benjamin. They're interested in finding him too."

Garrick sat in his chair and folded his arms. With a nod, he encouraged Wilkes to continue.

Wilkes cleared his throat. "Well, sir, when you flashed his face up at the press conference, it jogged a couple of memories. Two witnesses thought they'd seen him three days before our first murder. They reached out to Tonbridge who are directly dealing with an armed robbery."

Garrick gave an involuntary gasp. "Armed robbery! And he's a suspect?"

"The witnesses *think* he, or somebody like him, held-up a security truck on its way from the Securitas depot there."

The depot was an unmarked secure holding facility for the Bank of England. In 2006 it had the ignominy of being the target for Britain's biggest robbery when fifty-three million pounds was stolen. Thirty-two million of which was still missing.

Garrick was aware of the heist, and glad he wasn't involved with the case. Dealing with criminal gangs was often worse than murder.

"How much was stolen?"

"It was a scheduled delivery for two million–"

"Two million quid?" Garrick barked.

Wilkes held up a cautionary finger. "But there was a last-minute schedule change. So there was only, ha, *'only'*, eighty thousand loaded." Wilkes laughed, then immediately regretted it under Garrick's withering look. He composed himself. "Two people armed with shotguns took the money minutes after it left the depot. They fled on foot. Oscar Benjamin fits the description of one man seen pulling his mask off a couple of streets away."

"We need to bring Rebecca Ellis in for formal questioning," said Chib.

Garrick was undecided. "Not yet. She's concealing something from us. She may not have been in the country during the robbery or the murder at Fraser's place. Yet everything seems to orbit around her." Talk about a *femme fatale*, he thought. It was becoming clear she was mixed up with Oscar Benjamin's illegal activities.

"If you find that interesting, then you will love this," said Chib, looking up from a message on her phone. "The owners of Rebecca's Airbnb live in Italy. They say the property was booked for four weeks. By Oscar Benjamin."

THE SCENT of the trail was getting stronger and with it fragments of the case were beginning to form a coherent picture for Garrick. Unlike the Hoy masterpieces. With the threat of Rebecca leaving the country soon, they had started the wheels in motion to get a search warrant for her Airbnb. As it had been booked and paid for by the very man they were looking for, he felt confident that it would come through quickly. Until then, the priority was establishing a connection between Ellis, Kline-Watson, and the first victim.

Instinct told him that there was one, but the connections were too vague. Whispers in the darkness that he couldn't quite link. Unlike earlier, he was feeling sharp and alert. In fact, he was feeling better than he had done in a long while. Perhaps the benefits of taking the sleeping pills?

At a set of traffic lights, he found Wendy's number on his phone and his finger hovered over it. It wasn't too late, so perhaps they could get a drink? Although she would have an early start at the school tomorrow, and after a day rambling, she may be exhausted...

Garrick stopped himself. He was making excuses. Something he'd been doing too much lately. He had to be more proactive.

The light turned green, and he turned towards Derek Fraser's hotel. There was being proactive; and there was putting work aside. He could only do one at a time.

Asking for Fraser at the front desk, he was guided into the hotel bar. Fraser was perched on a stool, waving animatedly as he talked to a woman. Jacketless, he had opened the top two buttons of his shirt. For him, that amounted to being casually dressed. As Garrick neared, he spotted an open champagne bottle cooling in an ice bucket and, from his slurred speech, it wasn't his first.

"Mr Fraser!"

Derek Fraser's smile slid into an open look of disgust. "Bloody hell! Can't a man have a celebration with a young lady?"

His companion was Molly Meyers. She was smiling, but her eyes sparkled with relief that Garrick had arrived to save her.

"Molly. Pursuing another scoop?"

"Mr Fraser has just sold two more Hoys. Hence the celebration."

"And you have a private interview?"

"Of course. Which was just ending," she said with some relief as she slipped off the stool and took her coat draped on the seat next to her.

"Oh! Stay darling. I got so much more to tell you."

Her smile never faltered. "I have everything, Mr Fraser. You've been wonderful. But I need to get my copy written up or you won't be in the paper."

Garrick smiled to himself. That was the perfect ammunition to cool Fraser's libido. She flashed a look of thanks at Garrick and quickly hurried out. With undisguised lust, Fraser watched her go.

"What an arse."

Garrick never took his eyes off the Scotsman. "I was thinking the same thing." He sat on Molly's stool. "Mind if I ask you a few questions?"

Fraser emptied his glass. He filled it from the bottle. It didn't quite reach halfway before the last drop.

"Oops. I'd offer you one, but you're on duty."

"Congratulations. The buyers found you after all?"

Fraser held up one finger. "Buyer. Singular and loaded. Went up to..." he used both hands to play a drumroll on the bar, "four-hundred thousand!" His voice dropped to a whisper. "And best of all, no commission!"

"Lucky for you, Mark isn't around anymore."

"Thirty per cent saved! I mean, don't get me wrong, he was a nice bloke. And a hundred-and-twenty grand will buy some bloody nice flowers. It'll also buy me a plane when I get me licence." With a hint of melancholy, he watched the bubbles rising in his glass. "And I've got another pair heading to the market soon. But I might give it a couple of weeks before announcing that." He put his finger over his lips. "Ssshhh! Even our little Molly tight-arse doesn't know about those. I'll get her out for dinner then."

"I thought you'd be happy to hear that we can let you return home in a day or so. Forensics have done all they can there."

"Terrific. About time."

"What has Rebecca said about it?"

"Mmm?"

"The house. She was expecting it as per your divorce settlement."

"Well, that cat's out of the bag now. She knows she's getting nothing. She threatened to sue me. I told her to go to hell." He chuckled. "She wasn't too happy about that either."

"Another two Hoys. He's knocking them out quickly."

Fraser's voice dropped to a whisper. "They're in me room. Ssshh!"

"You met today?"

Fraser sipped the champagne. "We had a rendezvous. You know, I never really liked champagne. Never saw the point of it."

Garrick mentally kicked himself. If he had assigned some protection to Fraser, then they would have been able to identify the elusive artist.

"You promised you would pass my questions to him."

"Aye, I did. When I have the answers, I'll let you know."

"Can you think of any time Rebecca and Mark Kline-Watson would have been in touch with each other before she entered the country?"

He watched Fraser gently roll the stem of the champagne

glass between his thumb and fingers, swirling the alcohol one way, and then the other.

Finally, Fraser spoke. His voice low, carrying a trace of regret – or was it fear? "Mark was broke. He put a lot of money into that gallery, but his tastes were all over the place. He asked me to help him out. I couldn't." His eyes glazed, and for a moment Garrick thought he was going to sob. "I haggled hard over his commission, but I let him have a bit more than I was comfortable with because I knew it would help him out." He took another sip of champagne. "Who would've thought Hoy would have taken off like that?" He snorted with disbelief. "Not me or I certainly wouldn't have given him thirty bloody per cent. So, when they exploded," he stabbed his thumb into his chest, "because of all my hard work setting the scene. Building the legend. He comes back to me and asks for more. Sixty per cent. Sixty!"

"And you told him where to go, in your inimitable way."

Fraser knocked back the champagne and hung his head. "I wanted to. The problem was that he had the network. All the buyers."

"They would find you anyway. You have the artist."

"I wasn't thinking straight. I felt like he had me over a barrel. Y'see, I made the mistake of telling him that Becs had cleaned me out. Taken all my liquid assets and ran off with a man who hated me guts."

Fraser wiped a tear from his eye and sucked in a deep breath. The cocky shyster that Garrick was used to dealing with was now a vulnerable man.

"Mark knew what buttons to press to get at me. There is only one person who could have told him that."

"Rebecca."

Fraser nodded. "I bet he reached out to her and she and

that meathead boyfriend of hers concocted a scam to discredit me." He gestured to the barman for the bill.

In the silence that followed, Garrick digested Fraser's words. They echoed the same line of enquiry he was following. And yet...

"What made you get in touch with Mark in the first place? It's a small gallery in Rye. And you said his tastes were dubious."

Fraser signed the bill without checking it. "I'm not stupid, Detective. I approached some better names than him in London. They either didn't think much of the work, or they didn't think much of me. It's a snooty world, the art world. A working-class kid from Glasgow doesn't fit in. Then I remembered Terri had sold a few of her pieces to him. He sold them for twenty quid, which at the time was a fortune."

"Terri is an artist? I thought she just studied it."

"She thought she could do it. But she was wrong." Fraser stood and swayed. "Now you have chased the skirt away, I might as well hit the sack alone." He motioned for the exit.

"One thing still baffles me. Who gains by killing somebody doubling as you?"

"Probably the same person who gains for having me killed. Night."

Fraser shuffled from the bar. Garrick glanced at the bill before the barman pulled the faux-leather wallet away. He'd had half a beer and the bottle of champagne and left no tip. Something the barman noted with a scowl.

It was raining heavily when Garrick left the hotel. He pinched the collar of his Barbour tight as he jogged to his Land Rover. His impulsive detour had left it too late to call Wendy, and he now regretted making it. He was halfway to his car when he noticed a white Volkswagen Beetle parked next to his. Molly Meyers was behind the wheel, looking tiny in the car's spacious interior. Her face was illuminated by her mobile phone, on which she was rapidly typing. She smiled when she saw Garrick and lowered her window.

"Problem with the car?"

"No," she turned the phone screen in his direction. "I was writing the bones of my piece while it was still fresh in my mind. Thanks for saving me back there. He's a bit lecherous when drunk."

"All part of the service," he grinned.

"And I never thanked you for giving me the first question at the press conference. For what it was worth." She laughed.

Two compliments in one evening, thought Garrick. He must be doing something right. He opened his mouth to reply – when he noticed a black Hyundai parked several yards behind his own car.

Then there came the crack of gunfire. Two shots, crystal clear despite the rain pelting the surrounding vehicles. Next came a smash of glass from the hotel – followed by screams.

19

P eople were rushing from the bar and dithering in the lobby as Garrick pushed through, closely followed by Molly, who held her phone up to capture every moment on video. Garrick looked around for some hint about where the shots had come from. A young receptionist, her eyes wide in fear, recognised Garrick and pointed a trembling finger towards the staircase.

"Stay here!" he said to Molly and galloped up the steps two at a time.

The grand staircase in the centre of the room split in opposite directions, curving around bright pink walls before meeting at either end of the first-floor landing. Garrick was out of breath when he reached the top. Molly was right behind him when he suddenly stopped, and she cannoned into him.

"I thought I told you to stay?"

"I'm not a dog!" she snapped back. Her gaze was suddenly drawn to a man running towards them down a corridor. He was clutching a handgun as he came to an abrupt stop when he spotted Garrick. He immediately turned around and sprinted back the way he came.

Garrick gave pursuit.

The man took a right down an adjoining corridor. Garrick's lungs were burning, his knees complaining, and a detached part of his mind was appalled by how unfit he was. He would never have lasted fifteen minutes on the ramble with Wendy.

His target jinked into the open door of a room and before Garrick knew it, he found himself in Fraser's large suite. The Scotsman was sprawled across the thick royal-blue carpet, groaning in pain.

The assailant hunkered in the frame of an open window. The curtains billowed as rain gust in from outside. The only light came from a table lamp, showing the man was wearing all-black, with a hoodie top pulled tight. The handgun was slipped in the belt of his jeans. A black face mask covered everything from his eyes down. He looked straight at Garrick – not with the eyes of a killer, but those of a frightened young man.

Then he jumped out.

"NO!"

Garrick darted to the window, unable to stop him.

The drop was only a few feet onto the angled glass roof of a conservatory, below which he could see the startled faces of diners peering up. The man slid on his backside towards the edge and fell the rest of the way onto the grass below.

Garrick wasn't thinking. He clambered through the window and onto the double-glazed glass panel. Only when he applied his full weight and heard it creak, did it occur to him he was several stone heavier than the other bloke. He twisted to turn back, but his shoes slipped on the rain-soaked glass and he fell flat on his chest. His palms squealed along the glass and refused to gain any purchase as he slid backwards.

Then he was suddenly flung off the edge. He landed on his feet – but momentum propelled him onto his backside, and he rolled across the slick grass, his breath knocked from him.

Clambering to his knees, he could just make out the figure disappearing into the dark grounds. With a snarl, primarily of self-loathing, Garrick clambered to his feet, ignoring the pains that seemed to come from every joint, and ran in pursuit.

The wet grass seeped into his shoes and socks, but it was the least of his discomforts. From some hidden reservoir within, Garrick gained a second wind and charged forward.

The man had slowed his pace as he glanced behind. He obviously hadn't expected the detective to follow because, even in the near-darkness, Garrick could see his eyes widen in surprise as he lunged into him. It had been a while since Garrick had played rugby in school, but he remembered how to tackle.

Both men crashed to the ground, sliding through the white H of a helicopter landing pad chalked on the grass. Garrick had weight on in his side and manoeuvred himself on top, reaching out to block a hand from clawing for his eyes. He felt nails dig into his cheek and draw blood. It was only at the last moment he saw the gun swing in from the other hand.

The cold metal slammed across his temple.

Everything started to spin – then he heard the deafening

crack of gunfire so close that a tinnitus whistle screech
through his ears. He couldn't resist as the man shoved him
off. Garrick's face pressed into the wet grass, his nose filling
with the scent of wet earth. He caught his breath as the whine
lowered into something a little less intrusive. He felt as if he
might vomit as he pushed himself upright. The spinning
motion settled, but it took him two attempts to stand on
wobbling legs.

The gunman had vanished into the darkness. Garrick
turned as a couple of people brave enough to investigate the
gunshot ran towards him. They were shouting, but the words
were muffled in his ears. They were led by the bobbing light
of Molly Meyer's phone.

UNIFORMED POLICE and a pair of ambulances were on the
scene by the time Garrick returned to Fraser's room. The
Scotsman was sitting on his bed, drinking a whisky offered by
the night manager and fending off the paramedics.

Garrick allowed the scratches on his cheek, and the
grazes on his temple, and hands, to be sterilised with a swab,
but other than that nobody had been injured. After
convincing the arriving police officers he was responsible for
the crime scene, he directed them to taking statements from
the rest of the guests. Throughout, Molly Meyers had
lingered quietly in the corner. Garrick had told her to leave,
but she had protested, pointing out that was no way to treat
anybody who had his back in the face of a gun-wielding
maniac. Plus, she was a witness. Garrick didn't have the
strength or patience to argue with her.

"When I got to me room, the door was ajar. I thought it
was housekeeping," Fraser reported between generous gulps

of whisky. However drunk he had been thirty minutes ago, the shock had sobered him up. "When I walked in, he was pawing over me art!" He indicated to his leather carry case propped against the wall. "I shouted – and then saw he had a gun. I threw the chair at him." He indicated to the wooden desk chair that was stuck part-way through a fractured windowpane. "He shot at me as I threw it. Then he shouldered past and out the door. I was terrified. I had only just got back to me feet when he barged back in again, waving his gun. He made it out of the window with you following."

"Has anything been taken?"

"No. Let's face it, we both know what he was after."

"Who knew you had them here?" Garrick glanced at Molly. "You said you hadn't even told her."

"Exactly!" snapped Fraser. "I told you I wanted police protection, and you didn't provide it!"

Garrick cast another look at Molly, who was intrigued by the unfolding story.

"You can't report any of this."

"Oh, I think I can."

"Not if it interferes with an active investigation."

"Then I'll tell people," growled Fraser. "I wasn't offered the protection I wanted and was then attacked."

Garrick's head was swamped by pain. He held up both hands, one to stop Molly, the other to silence Fraser.

"Of course we'll assigned somebody after this."

"And I don't want to stay here. I want me own house. I feel safer there."

Garrick didn't want to argue the point in front of Molly, especially as his home was the scene of the first murder. How safe could he really feel there?

"Not tonight."

"Then in a cell. Me and me art."

"You want to spend the night in a prison cell?"

"Unless you don't think I'll be safe there?"

Garrick could see he was being deadly serious. He nodded. "Okay, I'll lock you up you myself."

Fraser opened the bedside table and took out a phone charger and his passport.

"Did the attacker seem familiar to you?"

Fraser shook his head as he moved to the wardrobe. "Couldn't see much, but no. He was younger than me, I reckon. My height. Armed."

Garrick realised Fraser was packing his belongings. "Leave everything as it is. Forensics will want to sweep through it all. If he got to the paintings, they'll want to check for prints."

"Fine. But they can do that anywhere. That case is staying with me."

Garrick pinched the bridge of his nose as he turned to Molly.

"How much did you get on video?"

"The whole thing. Including your heroic leap out of the window." Garrick winced. He knew he would look a complete fool. "That's now evidence." He held out his hand for her phone.

"Of course. I've already emailed the file to you." She smiled sweetly. "I don't see how my phone is needed."

"And you can't show that to anybody."

She sucked in her breath. "Ah, sorry. If only you told me that earlier. The BBC has it too."

"Molly..."

She lowered her voice; her freckled face breaking into a cheeky smile. "This is career pay dirt for me. A chance to jump from a local paper to television!"

He had no right to stop her, but it was bloody galling that Fraser was once again going to be a media darling, and he was dragging Garrick with him.

20

Derek Fraser was the first person who Garrick had placed into a prison cell who was relieved to be there. Molly Meyer had pestered Fraser for an exclusive interview, which he had finally agreed to give from his cell, although Garrick suspected that he only wanted to hear her beg for the privilege. The press coverage was going to add to his own burgeoning legend.

Garrick's hand was still shaking by the time he reached home and stared at himself in the bathroom mirror. His left temple sported an angry red welt from where he'd been struck with the pistol. The scratches on his cheek were small, but vivid. They'd bled the most. His hands and forearms were blotched with grazes and bruises from his various falls, and when he twisted around, his back and buttocks were a patch-work of larger ugly purple bruises, making it uncomfortable to sit or lie down.

He desperately needed sleep but didn't dare take a pill because he had to be up in just a few hours.

Sleep never came.

He felt terrible by the time he reached the station. News of the previous night's incident was all over the early morning news, with Molly's video going viral. When he walked into the incident room, he was greeted with a round of applause from the few who had made it in early. From the BBC News website, Chib was playing Molly's footage of the assailant disappearing through the window and Garrick fearlessly charging after him. By the time Molly crossed the room and caught up with the camera, Garrick could just be seen disappearing over the edge of the conservatory. The darkness concealed his pratfall and preserved his dignity. The TV presenters were rich in their praise of the heroic police officer.

The image of the gunman was too blurry to provide a useful identification, and the hotel's security camera in the lobby, and one looking across the car park, had their wires snipped. The staff claimed they'd been intermittent for months since a new software update, so they'd thought nothing of it.

Fanta caught an update on the computer system. "Forensics say the bullets were blank 9 mm shells." She flashed him a grin. "Still, jumping out of the window was pretty awesome, sir."

"Blanks can still be lethal." Garrick didn't know why he suddenly felt the need to defend his actions. "And regardless, Fraser wouldn't have known either. It doesn't change the thief's motives."

His mobile rang. It was Wendy.

"You're on the TV again!" she squealed with delight.

"I noticed." He moved to a quiet corner of the room, which was becoming busier by the moment. His freehand covered his ear, and he lowered his voice.

"I'm dating a real hero! I don't know how I'm supposed to react to that. I suppose rambling isn't as exciting as chasing gunmen across rooftops."

"I will take a ramble with you anytime."

She tittered suggestively. "Ooh, detective..."

Garrick felt himself blush. God, he was feeling like a schoolboy. Or perhaps it was the lack of sleep and his jangling nerves.

"Maybe you can tell me all about it later tonight? Or at least as much as you can."

It was going to be a long day. He'd had no sleep, and he was feeling awful. He saw Superintendent Margery Drury marching into the room. She met his gaze and gave him a thumbs up.

"That would be great," he found himself saying. "Sorry, I have to go. Let's talk later."

"Take care, hero!" The spark of awe in her voice was alarming. He was concerned that he was setting her up for a massive disappointment. He pocketed the phone and clapped his hands to gain his team's attention.

"We need all hands for this." His eyes fell on Fanta who sudden sat upright, not quite believing him. "Including you. We have our search warrant. With any luck, this is going to slam the case closed."

TWO POLICE MERCEDES Sprinters skidded to a halt on the Airbnb's gravel driveway, followed by four marked police cars. They were running silent and, before the convoy stopped next to Rebecca Ellis's rented Fiat, six burly police officers in body armour had already piled from the Sprinters and were converging on the house. Four carried Heckler &

Koch MP5 semi-automatic carbines, while another lugged a heavy red steel enforcer battering ram.

"ARMED POLICE!" they yelled as they reached the door.

Garrick and Chib watched from the back of the lead marked car. Fanta sat in the front seat, fingers gripping the dash as she watched the battering ram smash against the front door's lock. It took three hard whacks before the wood around the lock splintered. A further strike was required to force it to swing open.

The four armed officers hefted their weapons and slipped inside in one fluid motion. They could hear the muffled shouts from within the building, then it fell silent. Garrick's anxiety rose as, for two minutes, nothing happened. Then the two unarmed officers who had waited outside quickly dashed in. Moments later they escorted a dazed Rebecca Ellis out. She wore trainers, grey jogging slacks, and had her distinctive long red coat draped over her shoulders. She was taken to the back of a police car and cast a scowl in Garrick's direction as he climbed from his vehicle and stretched his sore back. He waved to a liveried Volkswagen Crafter van parked near the gate. It was marked DOG SECTION. In moments, the trained handlers leashed up a pair of keen sniffer dogs, immediately sending the German Shepherds searching across the drive.

Garrick led the way inside the house, Fanta, Chib, Wilkes and Lord following. They split to search the separate rooms they'd been assigned to. Garrick joined the armed officer standing in the living room who was watching the muted BBC rolling news playing an on enormous projector screen. He held his rifle in a low carry position and gave Garrick a curious look as he recognised him from the telly.

"Wouldn't mind one of these myself," said the officer, nodding to the screen.

"Did she resist? Or say anything?" Garrick looked around the luxurious living room, noticing the BBC report was showing the footage of him in the hotel. Feeling awkward, he didn't meet the officer's gaze. There was a half-eaten bowl of cereal on the table, that had turned into a soft mulch in a puddle of milk. Next to it was a still-steaming cup of tea.

"No. She was crapping herself."

Garrick saw an Alsatian being led into the spacious mani-cured rear garden. He crossed into the open-plan kitchen. It looked barely used. There were two cups in the sink; only one had a lipstick mark on the rim.

Chib hurried down the staircase and Garrick joined her in the hallway. "Looks like one person slept in the bed. I can't see any obvious signs of anybody. And we can't find those holdalls she picked up from Matthews."

Garrick nodded. He walked back outside and saw Sean Wilkes had all the doors of her Fiat Panda open and was examining the boot. The car carrying Rebecca Ellis drove away, passing a white forensics van that was turning in from the main road. He wished he wasn't feeling so fatigued and didn't trust himself not to fumble over some small pivotal clue. This was where all the threads had led. This is where he'd find the answers.

THE INTERVIEW HAD SCARCELY BEGUN when Rebecca Ellis slammed both hands on the desk and shrieked at Garrick.

"This is a ridiculous waste of time! Instead of dragging me in here, you should be out there finding my Oscar!"

For a moment Garrick was thrown, although he was careful not to show it. It wasn't quite the line of defence he'd been expecting. She was either a very good actor or was genuinely upset. He couldn't tell which.

"I think you know where he is."

"If I knew I wouldn't be in this sinkhole of a country, would I?"

"What was his business here?"

"I told you already. I don't know. I never asked questions."

"Because it was illegal?"

The suited lawyer next to her shook his head. "Don't answer that."

"No! We have a relationship in which we respect each other's privacy." She folded her arms and tilted her chin defiantly.

Garrick pushed across the photograph of her and the mysterious person loading the bags into her car.

"Help me with a name."

Rebecca looked at them for longer than necessary. She picked it up and held it closer. "That's an old friend I hadn't seen for a while. She was passing through, so we caught up. I gave her a lift to Ashford International. It gave us a chance to catch up."

A woman? That wasn't what Garrick had hoped for. At the back of his mind, he'd matched the height of last night's gunman with the figure in the photo.

"We'll need her details."

"Jenny Laverty. She's in France now. She could be anywhere. I don't have any details to give you. She said she'd reach out to me when she settles down."

"This Jenny, did you take her back to the house for a catch up?"

"There was no time. I left you, picked her up at Tonbridge

where she was going to change for Ashford. It made sense to meet her there. It was short and sweet."

Changing trains made sense. That was another disappointment.

"Oscar rented the house you're staying in."

Rebecca shrugged. "Which is why I'm staying there. No big mystery."

"We didn't find any of his clothes or belongings."

Rebecca managed a sarcastic smile. "Bravo. Now you see why I'm so concerned about finding him. When I arrived, he'd taken everything. He always travelled light, but he'd taken his shower gel, shaver, blood pressure tablets. All gone. Which is why I'm so worried."

Her voice faltered slightly. Garrick was starting to believe her. Or at least that side of her story. He produced the photo DC Liu had taken, showing her arguing with Mark Kline-Watson. She looked at it, then at him.

"I'm having déjà vu. Didn't we have this discussion already? Voluntarily? And without my solicitor?"

"For the record, and for your solicitor's benefit..."

"I was there because I wanted to contact Hoy, because I believe my ex-bastard husband kept his business interest a secret to avoid splitting everything in the divorce."

"And you believed Mr Kline-Watson when he said he had no contact with Hoy?"

"It fits with Derek's obsession with secrecy and his desire to be at the centre of the universe."

"Who do you think killed him?"

The solicitor sighed. "Detective, you can't put words in my client's mouth."

Garrick raised an eyebrow at him. "She can pick any name she wants. Who do *you* think killed him?"

The solicitor, whose name he had blanked the moment they were introduced, was taken aback. "My opinion has nothing to do with anything."

"Noted." He looked at Rebecca. "And your opinion is?"

"Derek. As I said already, he has everything to gain."

"And who has to gain if Derek Fraser ends up dead? You are aware somebody shot at him last night?" He decided she didn't need to know about the blanks.

"So I discovered this morning, watching TV. Just before you kicked my door down. And again, I thought we'd covered this when I willingly cooperated with you. He lied about leaving the house to me. What else has he lied about? And what do I stand to gain except a costly legal probate?"

"Who could he have passed the house onto?"

She gave a bewildered look. "He has no family, no friends. Half the people he knows hate him; he hates the other half."

Garrick was worried. Her reactions perfectly mirrored his own doubts and thoughts. She had an answer for everything – except the most pressing one.

"Did you know Oscar Benjamin is wanted in connection to an armed robbery in Tonbridge the week he arrived?"

She looked shocked. "No. That's rubbish. He wouldn't..."

Garrick chuckled. "Come on. He is no saint, and I don't believe for a second you are so naïve not to know about his reputation."

"His *brother's* reputation. Not his. He took all that crap from Noel and from Derek. Show me his criminal record." She smirked and stabbed a finger at Garrick. "Exactly! You can't because he is a good man."

Garrick propped his elbows on the table and leaned forward, softening his voice. "I can see you're concerned. You understand that he's wanted for questioning in connection to the murder at Fraser's house *and* an armed robbery. That's some achievement for an innocent man who has been in the country for three weeks, and it's an even greater achievement for his brother who is still behind bars. And I can't believe that he may have fled with the money, with no intention of ever returning to you." She reacted to that; it hadn't occurred to her. Garrick tried not to smile. "Yet, no matter how much you try to convince me he was a caring, lovely bloke who liked puppies and rainbows, I won't believe a single word of it until I speak with him. Where is he?"

She leaned forward, mimicking Garrick's pose. She lowered her voice. "I don't know. And if you want to play the dickhead game, he's allergic to puppies."

"What a bloody infuriating woman!" he bellowed across the incident room.

Wilkes and Chib had arrived back from Rebecca's Airbnb, leaving Fanta and Harry to finish things up. So far, the frustrating news was they had found nothing incriminating. Forensics were still doing a sweep, but they could tell it hadn't been used much over the rental period.

Raiding the house was now looking like a bad idea after all. He could already envisage the flak he was going to get from Drury.

"There is some bad news," Wilkes said jocularly.

"That was the good news?" exclaimed Garrick.

"The press arrived quickly." He jerked a thumb towards the door. "They're also laying siege outside, so I wouldn't show your face if you can help it. Unless you can do a little smoke and mirrors and throw them off the scent." He caught Chib's frown. "I saw a magic show on Friday..." he hesitated, unaware if she knew who his date had been. "And we, I, bumped into the DCI. It was a good show..." he trailed off.

"Smoke and mirrors," Garrick echoed. "That's what this feels like. Look over here while something else happens over there." He waved both hands to make his point. He walked to the evidence board. "We are missing somebody. If, for the sake of argument, Oscar Benjamin was robber number one. Even if he was doing it as a sideline while trying to help Rebecca Ellis find Hoy, so she could screw over Fraser. Who was robber number two?"

Chib beamed at him. "Tonbridge have no leads. And with no car used in the escape, they have no prints either. But you beat me to my surprise." She couldn't stop smiling at Garrick's baffled look. "Forensics came back with a match on the gun used last night. The blanks and the live shells fired during the Tonbridge robbery, came from the *same* weapon."

21

Hard evidence linking the cases had buoyed Garrick's jaded spirits and banished the fatigue that had been clawing at him all day. Even when Harry and Fanta had returned with no more news from the Airbnb, he remained optimistic.

Towards the end of the day, he received an unexpected call from Derek Fraser thanking him for being allowed to return home, and for placing a uniformed officer in a car at the end of his driveway. The sceptic in Garrick thought that his heartfelt outpouring was more to do with the fact he'd yet again been a media darling as he recounted his near-death experience. He'd used the opportunity to announce that it had happened with two more new pieces of artwork falling into his possession and, like the showman he was, he added further petrol to the story by suggesting that Hoy may be cursed. Rather than put buyers off, it seemed to have the perverse effect of attracting them to the works. Why spend money on an ordinary painting, when you could have one with links to the supernatural?

Forensic evidence showed the gunman had fled using a car parked in a country lane behind the hotel. It was probably the way he'd gained entry too. Garrick had asked for security footage of everybody entering the orthodox way prior to the video cameras being sabotaged. If the gunman hadn't cut them himself, then he must have had an accomplice on the inside. Garrick looked at the footage of everybody coming and going until the two key cameras went dead, but nobody leapt out as a possible suspect. As he'd only seen the man's eyes and had a sense of his general height and build, he had little to go on, but everybody caught on camera seemed too old, tall, small, or fat.

He also noticed that the cameras had been cut before the black Hyundai arrived.

By the time it reached five o'clock the team drifted home. All of them were exhausted. Except Garrick. He called Wendy and noticed that he had three missed calls from Molly Meyers, who'd also made capital by appearing as a guest on various news channels. He suspected it wouldn't be long before the job offers followed; she was photogenic, articulate and savvy. It felt like the only people not yet benefiting from the case were Rebecca Ellis and himself.

THE PIZZA HUT in Gillingham was not exactly a glamorous location, but Wendy had been excited when he suggested they meet there. She greeted him with a big hug and a short, but passionate, kiss. She gently rubbed the scratches on his cheek. Then the red welt on his temple which had almost vanished save a red blotch.

"You've been in the wars."

When he told her that if they had sat at the Pizza Hut in

Maidstone they'd have been assaulted by the press, Wendy had almost bounced in her chair with delight. She demanded to hear everything about the encounter, and listened with wide adoring eyes, barely even noticing when their twelve-inch Hawaiian Pizza and the garlic bread side arrived.

"I have to admit, I sort of told *everybody* in school that we were dating."

"Oh... poor you."

"They were impressed. I never really thought about your job as being dangerous. I mean, it's not like the police on the streets."

Garrick stopped himself from wolfing down the pizza. He'd eaten little all day, and he was finding the combination of Wendy's company and her adoration to be an addictive cocktail.

"Normally it's not. Not really. I turn up when the danger has already passed. To be honest, most killers give up at the end and don't put up a struggle." He decided she didn't need to know about fighting his old friend as his shop burned down around them. He'd also edited out the fact the bullets had been blanks; the team wanted to keep that quiet for now. He felt a little guilty that it was making him appear far braver than he had been.

She reached across the table and took his hand. Squeezing it, she didn't let go.

"It still made me realise what we have and..." she seemed lost for words.

Garrick suddenly had the unprovoked thought that she was about to dump him. As a younger man, pounding the streets as a PC, he'd had a series of short relationships with women who loved a man in uniform, but drew the line about getting involved with somebody who flirted with danger. Poor Wendy didn't even have the benefit of the uniform.

She continued. "And it suddenly felt precious." She flashed a lopsided grin, then let go of his hand and covered her face in embarrassment. "Wow. I sound like one of those cheesy Hallmark movies."

Garrick didn't know what she meant but played along anyway. "No, you don't."

"I just mean that I joined *Heartfelt* because I needed a change in my life. My job is dull and repetitive. Although I love the kids."

"You keep saying." As a teaching assistant she was increasingly frustrated at work but stopped short of suggesting that she could do better than half the teachers in the school, although Garrick suspected she was more than capable.

"But now I'm dating an actual action hero, it puts my boring life in perspective."

His relationship muscles were so badly tuned that he wasn't sure how to respond. "Sorry?" He was relieved when she smiled.

"Don't be. You're that welcome relief I needed in my life."

Garrick beamed with pleasure. He was starting he feel the same about her, although he hoped it wasn't just because she'd spent the entire time over pizza and a chocolate sundae, which they diligently shared, telling him how wonderful he was.

The moment was spoilt when Garrick caught movement out of the corner of his eye. A gaggle of Millennials seated at a table opposite were hunched conspiratorially together and casting looks his way. The furtive movement that caught his attention was one of them angling their phone for a photograph. A spotty, thin-faced man broke ranks and approached their table.

"Excuse me, mate. Are you that copper from the telly?"

Garrick treated him to a lazy smile. "Poirot? I get that a lot."

The gag passed in orbit over the young man's head. "From the news?"

"Not me. Sorry."

The man retreated to his table, but obviously wasn't buying it. Some of his friends were already Googling the story and nodding.

"Time to go," Garrick said, burning with embarrassment.

Wendy was quiet as they strolled across the car park. Something was on her mind. They reached her car when she finally spoke up.

"It's a bit of a disappointment to call it a night so soon. Want to maybe get a coffee?" Then after an awkward pause, "Back at mine?"

Garrick screamed at himself for hesitating, but the offer coincided with a sudden crashing wall of fatigue as the last two days caught up with him.

She playfully toyed with the collar of his Barbour, straightening it. "I just remembered that you don't drink coffee. I'm sure I have something much more to your tastes."

"I'd love to, Wend. But I haven't slept at all..." His bumbling apology sounded like the death knell to his manhood. And he didn't know where *Wend* had suddenly sprung from.

"Oh. That's okay. I'm sure it's been a mad few days." She awkwardly thumbed her key fob and unlocked the car.

"I mean between last night and this morning, I only had a few hours–"

She silenced him with a crushing hug, wrapping both arms tightly around him. Every bruise on his body screamed, but he got away with a strained gasp.

"Next time," she said and planted a lingering kiss on his lips. Her tongue gently sliding against his. She smiled and slipped into her car without another word.

Garrick ran his hands across his stubbled cheek as he watched the red tail lights recede into the distance. She had left him with a promise of so much more... if only he could stay awake.

DAVID GARRICK CUT the engine to his car, but left the head-lights on, illuminating his front door. He'd driven home on autopilot, having no recollection of the trip. He recalled watching Wendy leave, then getting into his own car, but precious little else.

Just how tired was he?

He ran a tentative hand over the top of his head, half expecting to feel the growth pressing from within. Of course, he felt nothing, nor did he feel the familiar nagging migraine. His doctor had warned him to avoid banging his head, whether it be on a football or his bed's headboard. Tumbling off rooftops was probably higher up the list than either of those. His eyes were dry and sore, and when he closed them, he could feel the welcoming embrace of sleep beckoning him. He turned the headlights off, locked the car and walked to the house.

He raised his key to the lock and stopped. The front door was ajar.

Was it an illusion created by the shadows? No. Only frac-tionally, by half-an-inch, but it was undoubtedly open. He swapped the keys for his phone and activated its LED torch. His heart felt as if it had leapt into his throat as he studied the lock. There was no sign of tampering. He gently applied pressure... and heard a click as the Yale catch slid off the strike plate. It hadn't been fully pulled closed to allow the lock to snap in position. Had he done that in his haste to leave in the morning?

As quietly as he could, Garrick entered the house and swept the light around. Nothing seemed to be disturbed. He suddenly realised how pointless it was using the phone; the darkness would only benefit an intruder. He reached for the light switch. Everything looked normal. His front door led directly to a staircase, with the living room beyond. His television was still there. The kitchen was undisturbed, with his laptop next to his fossil project.

A quick check upstairs assured him that nothing had been taken. The partially open door was due to his own carelessness. Now the adrenaline rush he had experienced had now woken him up once more.

"Pull yourself together, David," he said to the house at large. Despite the frustrations of the case, he detected an undercurrent that the universe was pulling at various strands of his life to make things go right for once. For the first time, he felt *he* was the one impeding his own success.

Wired and alert, he retired to bed and submitted to the sleeping pills.

22

The gun had been found by National Rail workers performing essential maintenance on the line in the dead of the night. DS Okon had arrived at the scene, parking on a bridge on Bowley Lane that crossed over the track. It was an obvious assumption to make that the gunman had driven at speed over a bridge two-hundred feet further down the road, passing over the M20, which would have been lit up at night. The rest of the lane ahead would have been smothered in darkness, so a person in panic may think they were tossing the weapon into a ditch. Not off another bridge and onto a dark railway line.

Forensics came back with a quick match: it was a silver Colt M1911A1 semi-automatic pistol. Forty years old and in a shoddy state, but it was still lethal. And it was the weapon used in both the security van robbery and the hotel incident.

It never ceased to amaze Garrick how villains could spend months or years concocting elaborate plans, then panic and make foolish errors, such as discarding a weapon in panic. He recalled the fear in the gunman's eyes. On reflection, it was as if the man hadn't expected his plan to go so awry. There was also the issue of why use live rounds attacking the security van, but blanks in the hotel.

Forensics discovered skid marks as the driver had slowed down to toss the gun, indicating he was alone. The same skid marks were found at the end of the lane, turning right at speed onto Lenham Heath Road. That gave them a direction of flight. It also provided a distinctive tyre tread pattern: they were *Bridgestone Turanza T005s*. Garrick launched an immediate search for any matching tyres fitted to a black Hyundai. The car that had followed him from Rebecca's Airbnb, probably the same one that was parked outside the hotel on the night of the shooting. Checks had revealed that it didn't belong to any of the hotel diners, guests, or staff.

Further research revealed that the black Hyundai that had followed them from the Airbnb had been parked in the owner's driveway in Guildford all week. The licence plate had been cloned. Was it the gunman's, or a persistent reporter? Garrick's suspicious mind jumped immediately to Molly Meyers, but he'd been with her when she was sitting in her Beetle.

The gaggle of reporters lurking outside the station had dwindled as the news cycle moved on. The video of Garrick sliding off a roof could only keep people amused for so long, but he was left in no doubt that the press was eager to leap on the slightest scent of blood in the story. Drury had taken him aside to confirm this.

"We're looking good on this case," she had said without a smile. "For a change. Mainly because of your little stunt and Mr Fraser's constant addiction to a camera lens. And how you've turned little Miss Molly Meyers onto our side, I can't imagine. She's been a pain in the arse since I first met her.

The sort of person who would flip a turd over to see if it's dirtier on the other side."

Garrick was impressed with the goodwill they'd been receiving from all quarters, despite their slow progress on the case. Drury's lofty tone tightened as she focused on just that.

"However, if we have nothing to charge Rebecca Ellis with, then smashing into her house at the crack of dawn won't look so diligent. And she is exactly the type of person who'll make a noise to discredit the investigation. And you, especially."

Garrick had been relishing the sense of momentum in the air, but her warnings pulled him back to earth. By lunchtime, Fanta had unearthed some details that warranted another interview with Rebecca Ellis.

Rebecca had slept well in her cell and now had changed her clothes and tied her hair back. She was composed compared to the previous day. A ghostly mocking smile lingered, powered by the certainty they had nothing to charge her with.

"How many visitors have you entertained at your rental?"

"I haven't been in an entertaining frame of mind."

"And your friend, Jenny..." he made a pretence as forgetting her surname.

"Laverty."

"You took her directly to the train station?" Rebecca nodded. "Only Eurostar have no passengers registered by that name."

Rebecca didn't flinch. "She must have used her maiden name on her passport."

"And what would that be?"

Rebecca shrugged. "I've only known her by her married name."

"Interesting. And how does using her maiden name affect her first name? Y'see, there was only one Jenny, or Jen or Jennifer, registered as a passenger all day. I'm as surprised as you. It is quite a common name. And that Jenny went to Disneyland with her husband and two children."

Garrick was delighted with how thorough Fanta had been in drilling down into the details. She even knew which hotel they were staying at. And she had gone further.

"And CCTV doesn't show you dropping her off at the station." He spread his hands. "I'm confused."

To her credit, Rebecca's smirk only slightly drifted into mild irritation. "I didn't drop her at the station. I dropped her near the Outlet centre. She wanted to pick up a few things before she left."

The Designer Outlet was an elliptical complex of about seventy stores, selling mostly out of season fashions at low prices. From a distance, the rooftop looked like a line of tents and always put Garrick in mind of an enormous circus. It was a popular destination for tourists and local bargain hunters alike.

"I see. Shopping?" He waited for Rebecca to confirm with a single nod. "Carrying those two big holdalls filled with her belongings?"

"If she was smart, she would've put them in storage."

"So, after saying goodbye, she went shopping, then failed to get on the train. A train which she didn't have a ticket for?"

"I'm not her mother. Maybe she had a change of heart? Maybe she lied to me?" She sighed and drummed her fingers on the table. "What else can I tell you? She was in a relation-ship she wanted to get out of. I never met him, and I don't know his name." She shrugged, end of story.

Garrick was impressed that she was keeping her cool.

"Maybe. Lies have a way of tripping people up." He let her fidget in silence, then toyed with the mug of matcha tea he'd brought with him. "Humour me. You had no visitors at the house."

Forensics reported a few indicators of other people, but as a rental that was to be expected. They had jokingly commented that it should get an extra star on its TripAdvisor rating because it had been so thoroughly cleaned. But one thing hadn't been.

"There were two cups in the sink."

Garrick paused. Rebecca's lips parted, but then she had second thoughts on whatever she had been about to say.

"One had lipstick marks that match yours. The other had normal lip marks, but it wasn't you. Who was it?"

Rebecca folded her arms. "Why don't you tell me?"

It was a woman, that much he knew. Otherwise they were drawing a blank on anybody with a previous criminal record.

"I think it's your non-existent guest."

"That cup was dirty when I found it in the cupboard. In fact, there were several plates and a knife that hadn't been washed properly. I was livid. When you rent accommodation at that standard, you expect it to be hygienic."

The smirk had returned. Garrick knew she was lying. With the obsessive level of cleanliness they'd found, he doubted a few dirty cups would have survived unnoticed. Finally, he passed her a photograph of the Colt pistol.

"Does this look familiar? It's old I know, but..."

She gave it a cursory glance. "Why should it? I hate guns." After a pause she added, "How long do you expect me to be in here? My flight home leaves tomorrow."

Garrick didn't dignify her question with an answer. Something had just occurred to him.

"Cast your mind back to your argument with Mr Kline-Watson."

Rebecca rolled her eyes and sighed theatrically. "I've told you all I remember. I wanted to find Hoy. I wanted to screw my ex-husband over. And if there was a law against *that*, then you would be arresting over half the women in the country."

"Did you know what Mark Kline-Watson did before opening his gallery in Rye?"

Rebecca licked her lips. He hesitated, unsure where he was going. "No."

Garrick flashed a shark-like smile. "I do."

HE TOLD Chib to drop everything and drive him into London. He spent most of the journey silently piecing together strands of information. When they arrived in Camden Chib again found a free parking space where she could charge the car. She caught Garrick's look.

"You're seriously tempted to get one of these, aren't you, sir?"

"What? And join the twenty-first century driving a yogurt pot on wheels? Perish the thought."

They rang Terri Cordy's doorbell, but she didn't answer, so they found a window seat in a Starbucks across from the street and waited. Chib ordered a large mocha, while Garrick was content with a small green tea and a blueberry muffin that was far too big to be healthy. He outlined his thinking.

"I can't persuade Fraser to reveal Hoy's identity. They saw one another recently, but he still hasn't returned the questions I gave him. Rebecca told me she thinks they met while he was seeing Terri. Terri put Fraser in touch with Mark Kline-Watson. They are the two most likely to have met Hoy."

"But he didn't know Hoy's identity."

"That's what he told Rebecca. Let's face it, why would he give anything away when she came charging in? Fraser told me Mark was demanding a bigger percentage, and he had substantial business debts."

"But Fraser refused to budge."

"I don't blame him. But for me it proves that Mark K-W didn't know Hoy, or he would have gone to him directly."

"Only Fraser knows his identity."

Garrick pointed at Terri's flat above the betting shop. "So does she, whether or not she's conscious of it. If Mark didn't get them together, then Rebecca is right, and she did. We just need to jog her memory."

Fifty minutes later, Chib finished another coffee just as Terri returned to her apartment carrying her baby in a papoose. They gave her five minutes so she could settle the child down before they crossed the street and rang the bell.

Terri was not pleased to see them, and it took Garrick two attempts to persuade her to let them inside.

"I've only just got Ethan to sleep," she said, ushering them to the sofa.

Garrick glanced around, noticing most of the baby's belongings were now packed in cardboard boxes. A MacBook Pro laptop was open on the coffee table. Terri quickly closed the screen.

"We want to talk to you about Mark Kline-Watson." Terri's eyes darted around the room before she bobbed her head. "You remember him?"

"Of course," she sighed. "He ran a second-hand shop in Islington. He focused on artwork that came from people wanting to get rid of their junk. He occasionally displayed work from new artists too, but to be honest, the shop was a bit of a dive. More a collection of bric-a-brac."

"Can you describe your relationship?"

"I was studying art. He was selling it. Sort of. I noticed a few new paintings that I thought were quite good, so we got talking and became friends."

"Do you remember the names of any of those artists?" Terri shook her head. "And you two were just casual friends?"

Terri self-consciously combed a strand of hair around her ear and looked offended.

"Do you mean, was I shagging him?" she snapped.

Garrick shrugged. "I merely want to establish how it was between you."

Her tone was suddenly cold. "We were friends. Did Derek put you up to this?"

"What do you mean?"

She stood and paced the room. "From the moment I introduced them, Derek accused us of having an affair. No, not 'us', just me. He wouldn't say anything to Mark's face. Oh, no. He didn't want to upset him. But upsetting me was fine."

"Why would he think that?"

"Because he's a control freak! Derek Fraser has always been a manipulative bastard, but I didn't see that until I got pregnant. Then he started asking if it was Mark's."

Garrick tried to reconcile Fraser's claims that he'd given Mark a slightly bigger percentage to help him out, against Terri's accusations that he once thought Mark had been sleeping with her behind his back.

"Forgive me for asking, but Mark *isn't* the father?"

"I never slept with him!" she said, staring out of the window, visibly upset.

With a single look, Chib berated Garrick for his heavy-handed approach. He scratched his nose, feeling embarrassed.

"I'm sorry to have asked, but we need everything to be clear." He silently mouthed to Chib to continue the interview, then he stood. "May I use your bathroom?"

She didn't look at him. "Down the hall on the left."

Garrick walked past the bedroom. The door was slightly ajar, through which he could see a cot and a couple of cardboard packing boxes inside. He found the shabby bathroom and relieved himself. He could hear Chib and Terri quietly talking in the living room. From the sound of it, Terri seemed much more at ease talking to her. Garrick regretted his direct questions. He hadn't meant to upset her, and it was an unwelcome reminder that the newer generation of cops were a much more tactile, understanding breed. He'd always been critical of the emotionless policing of the eighties and nineties, now he was finding himself falling foul of similar criticisms. Maybe each generation of officers was becoming more understanding and gentler. He chuckled to himself. God help the ones coming in after Chib. They'd probably be so soft they'd want to hold counselling sessions with their suspects, just to make sure they didn't upset a murderer's feelings.

He zipped up his fly and flushed the toilet. Squirting the last dregs of soap from a plastic dispenser, he quickly washed his hands... then he noticed something draped over the radiator.

"Bloody hell..."

He took a quick photograph of it before hurrying back to join the women. He paused in the hallway to read a message from Fanta. She had details on Mark Kline-Watson's old shop in Islington. He glanced into the bedroom next to him as he heard the baby gurgle. He nudged the door a little wider until he could see movement in the cot. The lad was sleeping and gently rocking his legs back and forth. Garrick wasn't one to fawn over babies, but it made him smile.

Now he could see the packing boxes in the room were filled with clothes that had been hastily thrown in without care. He spotted a black holdall bag in the corner. Just like the ones he had seen Rebecca Ellis put into her car. They were common enough, but the coincidence rankled him.

It brought with it questions he hadn't considered. Had Rebecca and Terri seen one another recently? Fraser's affair with Terri was the reason for their divorce, so why would they? Was there some truth in Rebecca's statement about trying to help a friend leave her partner? Terri was clearly packing in a hurry and had been dismayed to see the police on her doorstep; then again, most people were. But if that was the case, why had Rebecca lied about her friend's identity?

He had a theory about that. One he was eager to share with Chib.

Garrick casually strode into the living room as Terri was reiterating how hard it was being a single parent.

"Well, thank you for your time, Terri. But please call us if you remember anything else about Mr Kline-Watson."

"I'm sure I won't."

Garrick tapped the top of a packing box. "Leaving soon?"

"As fast as possible out of this dive."

"Moving in with a boyfriend?"

She shot him a black look. "I don't have one. Not since that med student who won't leave me alone. I don't want him following me."

"Who is he?" asked Chib.

Terri shook her head. "A bloke from Canterbury. One of a string of bad mistakes." She cast a finger across the boxes. "That's all going into storage." She stopped herself from elaborating. "Then Ethan and I will find somewhere better than here. Anywhere, really."

They left Terri just as the baby woke and began to cry. It wasn't until they were several yards away that Chib spoke up.

"That was a brand-new laptop."

"I noticed. She was a little hostile over Mark K-W, I thought."

"You were a bit... clumsy, sir. Sorry."

Garrick waved a finger at her. "Don't you *ever* apologise for telling me your thoughts, Chib. Especially when you're right. Still, I'm not the dinosaur you think I am."

"I didn't mean—"

"Fanta discovered more about K-W's business in Islington. It's a Wine Bar now. But she found an archived website with some of the bric-a-crap he was selling. Artwork, furniture, a few antique odds and ends." She'd sent the weblink from the *Wayback Machine*, an online archive that attempted to capture the history of the internet by making snapshots of the ever-changing websites. They reach Chib's car and as she unplugged it, he held up his phone so she could see. "It seems the people of Islington had more taste than he did. He barely sold anything. But amongst the junk is something interesting. He sold antique firearms."

By law, old weapons had to be made safe before they could be sold on to the public. The modern methods employed rendered the weapons so useless that it would be easier building a gun from scratch than repair it. However, the Colt had been deactivated before the laws were tightened. Deactivation was achieved by drilling out the barrel and blocking it with a pin. It took a lot of effort to reactivate it, but it had the advantage of making the weapon almost untraceable.

He held the screen closer so Chib could see the image he had selected. It was a familiar-looking Colt pistol.

"Oh, wow. Could it be the same one?"

"They're trying to find that out. But what are the odds? What forensics can confirm is that the Colt we found had been deactivated around the same time. I'm betting it was the same weapon."

"So the odds mean Oscar Benjamin and Mark knew one another."

"Fraser and Rebecca connect them. They moved in the same circles, so it would be improbable if they'd never met. If Mark was so desperate to pay off his debts, when not sell some untraceable weapons that he may have lying around?"

They leaned on the Nissan's roof as they rallied the possibilities back and forth.

Chib nodded as she saw a plethora of connections opening. "If Rebecca knew what Oscar was planning, then it makes sense she'd go to Mark if she was desperate to find him. She had no interest in finding out who Hoy is. That's just a smoke screen."

Garrick held up a cautionary finger. "Perhaps that was the case, but this whole Hoy fever has whipped up from nowhere. Prior to the body in Fraser's living room, the world didn't care."

Chib ruminated on that. They opened the car doors and sat inside. The display panels silently came to life, and Chib set the satnav for the police station.

"Did you see what was on her laptop screen?" he asked.

"No. She was rather keen to close it."

"It was a passport application."

Chib was surprised. "That's what she means by wanting to leave."

"And," he jerked a thumb at himself, "this old Detective Rex may have figured out the question everybody is asking?" He flicked through the images on his phone and showed it to Chib.

"Why are you showing me a naff bathroom? If you're asking me to help with your DIY..."

"It's not my bathroom. It's Terri's. *Look*."

She stared and zoomed in on the damp towel draped across the radiator. Then she gasped. It was stained with multicoloured paint that had faded after a wash.

Garrick couldn't stop smiling. "How much does it change things if we have uncovered the identity of our phantom artist?"

23

"We have to release Rebecca Ellis tomorrow morning," Drury growled over the phone. "And by the afternoon, I imagine she'll be holding a press conference to turn this entire investigation against us."

"Maybe it would be better if we release her now, ma'am," said Chib into her car's hands-free.

Drury was in a tetchy mood. Garrick had learned to deal with it over the years, so he winced when Chib spoke up. She still had a lot to learn.

"How the hell does that help?" snapped Drury.

"She could lead us to Oscar Benjamin."

"If that was the case, she would've done that already. I've seen her type before. If you pepper the lies with enough truth, it becomes almost impossible to tell which is which. I don't trust her. As soon as she's out, she'll be on a flight home, and my money is Benjamin is already out of the country."

Garrick had been mulling over similar thoughts. These days, dealing with European police forces was more cumbersome that it had been, but that was down to paperwork. The flesh and blood officers at both ends were still keen to help one another. Still, a cross border case would protract everything.

He finished the call as quickly as he could. Chib looked sullen. "Don't let her get under your skin. She's a dragon. But there are plenty of times it's handy to have a dragon watching your back."

"She hates my ideas."

"She's probably peeved that she doesn't think of them herself. You know better than me what it's like being a woman on the force. Let's face it, she didn't get there by being a team player. She got there through sheer bloody-minded-ness. I'm under no illusion that this is the height of my career, no matter how bloody-minded I am."

I'm probably past promotion, he thought miserably. They'd left Camden riding high and feeling they had made some important links, but his mood had crashed back to earth when he listened to a voicemail from Dr Rajasekar, confirming that a slot for his next MRI scan was available. He deleted the message and felt nervous at the prospect, remembering his therapist's comment that ignorance is bliss. When had she said? Tomorrow? He made a quick note on his calendar. The message had made him feel drained. Drury's rant had merely melted the icing from his cake.

They headed back down the M20 towards headquarters, but Garrick was desperate to avoid going back. He felt there was more to achieve out here and considered paying Derek Fraser a visit just to see the look on his face when he revealed Hoy's identity. But, other than personal gratification, there was nothing to be gained from that, and if he knew that

Rebecca and Terri had struck up some sort of friendship, he would've revealed it earlier.

Try as he might, Garrick still struggled to find what bound the women together, other than loathing the same man. If Fraser was doing well selling the art, then it made little sense for Terri to ditch him as an agent. It was Fraser's own fame that was helping drive up the price. Instinct told him they were looking at the evidence the wrong way. Maybe he was being unduly influenced by Fanta's whimsical take on viewing artwork, but it was sticking with him. So had something else she had said... her date with Sean. The magician. Sean's smoke and mirrors comment.

"We're looking at the wrong hand," he said suddenly.

"Sir, you have well and truly lost me."

GARRICK HEADED to get to the incident room to access the case files. He stood in front of the evidence wall to soak it all in.

The second gunman at the security van incident had to be the same man Garrick chased in the hotel. The gun, and now the Mark Kline-Watson connection, put him by Oscar Benjamin's side. He knew he should inform the team investigating the robbery, but until he had something other than speculation, it was probably best to keep quiet.

It was likely that Oscar Benjamin had fled the country, leaving his partner in crime behind. Why? Had Benjamin stolen all the money from his partner? Left him high and dry? Had he done it to escape from Rebecca to start a new life? It was possible.

"Do you have a moment, sir?" It was Fanta, who was

leaning back in her seat. She had dark circles under her eyes, betraying her fatigue.

Garrick crossed over. "When did you last go home?"

"What year is it?" she quipped, then pointed to her screen. "What do you make of this?"

She scrolled down a series of bank statements showing thousands of pounds regularly coming in and out.

"My dad was an accountant in Shanghai before he came over," she said.

"Ah, the man who named you after a fizzy drink."

"I used to tell people it was short for Fantasia." The truth was that Fanta had been one of the few English words he'd remembered at short notice. "He used to teach me and my brother bookkeeping when we were kids."

"Wow. Your family nights in must have been wild."

Ignoring him, she circled the mouse cursor over the figures. "So even I can tell this looks dodgy. They're K-W's Islington business accounts prior to his business collapsing."

"He was making some quite substantial sales."

"Yeah. All very regular for somebody who, by all accounts, wasn't shifting much out of the store." She switched to a browser and called up the shop's old website on the *Wayback Machine.* "I trawled through this. For a year he had pretty much the same items on there. He'd tweak the prices to get rid of them, but look, month after month, it's mostly the same stuff. He might not have put everything on there, but this is the world's shop window. Surely he'd put up the big-ticket items. Look at this. It's a pink elephant!" She was indignant at a ceramic pink elephant, standing three feet high, with its truck reared back. "He was charging seven grand for that! Who would want it?"

"Isn't that what you consider art?"

"No. That's kitsch. And according to the website, nobody wanted it as it was still there until he closed. So where was he making the money?"

Garrick had seen similar set-ups before. "Money laundering."

Fanta leaned back in her chair and put her arms behind her head. "That's what I was thinking."

Garrick used the mouse to flick back to the bank statements. "He wasn't making a profit unless he was keeping it in cash as a backhander. The business was unsustainable, even as a front." He scrolled through the records. "These early figures seem normal. So maybe he was really trying to make an honest go of things, then found the path for easy money."

"Then he had to close."

"But couldn't risk applying for bankruptcy. That would affect what type of bank account he could later have. It would be too risky to have any bank closely monitor his activities, so it would be better for him to be in debt rather than write it off."

"The financials for the Cinq Arts Gallery follow a similar pattern, except this time with some profits sunk back into the business." Fanta's nose wrinkled as she thought. "It was another money laundering front."

"It certainly smells like it, doesn't it?"

"And it feels right that he'd try to squeeze more money from our man Fraser. If he could pay off his debts quick, it would open the doors for his business to legitimately shift larger amounts of money."

"The only problem is, we're now building a case against a victim. How does Rebecca Ellis tie into this?"

He outlined his thoughts on Oscar Benjamin's accomplice. Harry Lord had been listening from his own desk. He rolled his chair over to join them.

"When me and Sean were asking about Benjamin, remember they said he was recruiting for a job? If this was the Tonbridge heist, then would he really use strangers? People he didn't trust?"

Garrick shook his head but remained silent as he walked back to the evidence wall and took in each face in turn. He peered at the CCTV picture of Rebecca Ellis and her phantom friend loading her car up. He tapped the figure in black.

"This is Terri Cordy," he declared with confidence. "Rebecca spun a cock-and-bull story about some friend because she didn't want us to make any connection between them. Sean backtracked her movements to the station." He looked around. "Where is he?"

"Late lunch..."

"If she's coming from Camden, where would she get the train from?"

"London Bridge is the overground line," said Harry. "She could get the Northern Line from her flat to the station."

"Check with TFL. She must have bought a ticket, used her Oyster card, something." Garrick's mind was suddenly firing on all cylinders. He hadn't felt this alert for months. "She comes to Tonbridge to meet Rebecca Ellis. Why?"

He looked expectantly between Harry and Fanta. They gave sheepish shrugs.

"To move the money!" He tapped the photograph. "That's what's in the bags! She didn't bring them with her."

He was expecting a triumphant whoop from the others, but there was only doubt.

"Why...?" Fanta squinted at the board. "Aren't we saying Oscar Benjamin made off with the loot?"

"Maybe not all of it. And she just bought herself an expensive laptop." Garrick now doubted his own idea. What had started off sounding promising had just hit the rocks labelled *lack-of-evidence.* Yet, he was sure there were flecks of truth in there somewhere. Or was he just tangling himself up in false leads?

"Mmm, maybe your idea is not as stupid as it sounds," said Fanta thoughtfully. With her hands still behind her head, she slowly revolved three-hundred and sixty degrees on her chair. As ever, she was oblivious to her lack of work-place etiquette.

"You flatter me," Garrick said sardonically, but he saw she was chasing the same thread that was tantalising him. Then he got it. It was obvious. "The only reason for Terri Cordy to be there is if she was in on the whole thing. *Like Rebecca.*"

Fanta suddenly bolted upright in her chair as he latched on to his reasoning. "Because *she's* the one connected to the second gunman!" It came out in one fast squeal.

Garrick nodded encouragingly, then looked to Harry for confirmation.

"Does that sound completely mad?"

Harry nodded. "Yeah. But we've gone out to bat off madder ideas than that."

DC Sean Wilkes entered, clutching a plastic bag from Subway. He glanced around the room, picking up on the mood.

"Have I missed anything?"

Harry ignored him. "The only problem is, we don't know who he is."

Garrick smiled as Fanta dropped back in her chair, suddenly deflated.

"No. But we know *where* he is."

GARRICK LEFT with DC Harry Lord. He thought having a marked car, would be useful. Plus, if things were going to get physical, Harry was more than capable of fighting for them both. He left Chib to extract another interview from Rebecca Ellis, while DC's Fanta Liu and Wilkes put together as much background information as they could on their new lead.

Terri Cordy had let slip she was dating a medical student in Canterbury, and that meant he had to be studying at the Kent and Medway Medical School. Having no description or name left a lot of potential students to sift through. Although Garrick was convinced that he'd recognise those wide, frightened eyes again. And since they'd been up-close and personal, he had a good measure of the man's physical build. That ruled out the short, tall, fat, and thin students.

Fanta trawled through student's social media accounts, while Wilkes took the more formal avenue of calling the Dean and arranging a meeting.

THE UNIVERSITY OF KENT campus was on the northwest edge of Canterbury, bordering the countryside, as if a decision had been brokered by the founders to keep the students as far from the townsfolk as possible.

The campus was packed with students moving in between lectures. The marked police car and DC Harry Lord cutting a handsome figure, drew more than a few curious looks. A waiting receptionist hastily guided them into the Dean's office.

Professor Julian Anderson, BM BS, had an impressive CV, which Wilkes had recited over the phone. He was a well-regarded academic figure, and an active champion for diversity. Garrick had been expecting a stern, lanky man, not the pleasant, rotund, welcoming face and demeanour that greeted them. The professor sat behind his desk, anxiously circling his thumbs as he went through the niceties of offering drinks. Garrick got straight to the point. Although he couldn't specify the exact nature of the offense, Professor Anderson guessed at least part of it.

"I thought I recognised you from the telly. Well, needless to say that I don't think any of our students would be involved in such a crass thing. We are talking about some of the brightest minds in the country here."

"Of course not. But we need to eliminate suspects from our enquiries."

Garrick was constantly amazed how people thought intelligence somehow lessened a person's penchant for crime. In his experience it was cut down the middle, regardless of creed, colour, or sex. The only discrepancy he had discovered was that the thicker ones were more easily caught. He was equally surprised by how many people assumed 'eliminate for our enquiries' meant just that. Most of the time when Garrick mentioned it, it was to dig up as much dirt on the suspect as possible.

Eager to cooperate, Professor Anderson fetched his secretary o they could access the student records. Garrick sat at the desk outside with the receptionist, with Lord peering between their shoulders. They cycled through the profile pictures of male medical students. The chubbier ones were instantly dismissed, as were any non-Caucasians. But with no information regarding their height, Garrick worried they may have to resort to an ID parade.

"Do students require a parking pass?"

"Yes."

They searched for any registered black Hyundai. There were two. Only one was a Hyundai i40, registered to Huw Crawford, a 32-year-old mature student. Checking the timetables, his lecture was ending at this very moment.

IT WAS EASIER to find the Hyundai in the car park than it was to filter everybody coming out of the lecture halls. Garrick and Lord were halfway across the parking bay when they spotted Huw Crawford. He was the right build. His black curly hair and dark stubble hinted at an Italian heritage rather than Welsh. He was too far for Garrick to confirm his identity – but Crawford had seen him first and bolted for his car.

"Wait!" Garrick shouted as he started forward - and ran straight into the side of a reversing Mini pulling out of the bay next to him. It was no worse than walking into a wall, but the young girl driving was already out and in tears as she repeatedly apologised. The impact winded Garrick, stopping him in his tracks.

"I didn't see you! Are you okay?"

Crawford was already in his car as DC Lord bolted towards him.

"Police!" he shouted unnecessarily.

Tyres shrieked on the wet asphalt as the Hyundai accelerated. Crawford had reversed into the bay, so now had a clear run out of the car park. He drove straight at Harry. There was a loud crump, and Harry tumbled across the bonnet. He slammed into the windscreen, the safety glass transforming into a spiderweb of white cracks.

The impact rolled Harry onto the roof and pitched him off at an angle. Students screamed and hollered as he crumpled onto the bonnet of another parked car, setting off its alarm.

The young woman was still fawning over Garrick, oblivious to the chaos behind her. Garrick pulled her aside just as the Hyundai roared past, so close that the wing mirror cracked across his already bruised buttocks. Plastic and glass shattered as the mirror casing snapped free and tumbled across the floor.

Garrick watched helplessly as it sped from the campus. Then he turned and limped as quickly as he could to DC Harry Lord who was sprawled, bleeding and unmoving, across the bonnet of the car.

24

There was no doubt in DCI David Garrick's mind that Huw Crawford was the key to unlocking the case and now a huge manhunt was now under way for the student.

Harry had recovered consciousness as the Paramedics arrived. Blood poured from a gash on his forehead where he had struck the windscreen, and his right eye was swollen shut. Garrick had lost his temper when none of the students had volunteered any first aid.

"What sort of medics are you supposed to be?" he yelled at them, wondering if the first thing students were taught was the negative legal ramifications of helping patients. One woman eventually stepped forward and stemmed the bleeding, warning Harry not to move in case he had any spinal injuries.

Three uniformed officers had arrived and kept the students away from the collision site. One approached Garrick with the latest news on the radio: the Hyundai had been found five miles to the north, abandoned on the edge of Whitstable.

That told Garrick they were dealing with somebody prone to panic. Clumsily disposing of the Colt had been his first mistake. Running over his arresting officer was the nail in his coffin. Now abandoning his car in a rural area, with the sea to the north, meant he was hemmed in. Unless he stole a vehicle, but that required a skill set that Garrick was sure Huw Crawford didn't possess. The police helicopter had been deployed from Essex and would join the search in the next half-hour.

He called Chib and instructed her to bring Terri Cordy in for questioning immediately. Thirty minutes later, the caretaker of Crawford's student accommodation on Parham Road was opening it for Garrick and a uniformed policewoman. It was a well-maintained modern complex, and the room itself was a far cry from the squalid conditions Garrick had endured as a student. Boasting a double bed, integrated sleek white furnishings, and a small kitchen that was better appointed that Garrick's own.

Crawford appeared to be a tidy lad. Medical textbooks were stacked on his desk, with pictures of the Grand Canyon, Yosemite Park, and the Mayan Pyramids in Yucatan on his wall as inspirational post-graduation rewards.

With blue latex gloves on, Garrick opened the desk drawers. Amongst pens, a book of stamps, and several food delivery menus, he found a small cardboard carton of 9mm bullets. The crimped blue casing tips indicated they were blanks. There was no computer or phone, both of which he guessed Crawford had on him.

He emptied a small wastepaper basket on the kitchen's white worktop. Amongst the plastic wrappers, an empty packet of Monster Munch, and some fliers for various student nights, was a return train ticket to London including an all zones travel card for tube and bus. Garrick took a photo of it and told the policewoman to wait until SOCO arrived.

Rebecca Ellis was the next obvious candidate to grill, but he preferred to do that once they had Huw Crawford in custody, so he decided to pay Derek Fraser a visit. Instead of calling Fraser directly, he contacted the officer camped at the bottom of his drive to confirm Fraser was home.

During the fifty-minute drive to Tenterden, he answered a call from Molly Meyers, who'd discovered Garrick was at the scene of the hit and run. Naturally, she'd assumed it was part of the investigation and wanted the details. He didn't see the harm in her making more noise about the manhunt. The sooner they found Crawford, the better. He hinted at the student's involvement, but provided details about DC Lord's assault with as much graphic detail as he could muster.

As he'd hoped, he caught Fraser on the hop. His initial surprise gave way to a welcoming gesture into the living room.

"I feel safer now you're here," Fraser joked as he disappeared into the kitchen. "Coffee? Tea?"

"No thanks." Garrick was still pumped with adrenaline and feared that a tea would throw him over the edge. Fraser busied himself with a Nespresso machine, swearing when the capsule became stuck in the slot. Garrick stopped in front of the television. A huge square of the bloodied carpet had been cut out with some precision. "That will be quite the conversation piece."

Fraser joined him and nodded. "I plan to have something very nice in its place soon. Tell me, Detective. Just how safe am I?"

"I'm hoping, with a fair wind and a stroke of luck, you might be able to go out and socialise this evening without being assassinated. Although don't quote me on that."

"If I do, I'll wear a bulletproof vest." Fraser flopped onto the sofa; legs splayed in a picture of slovenly relaxation. He balanced the small espresso cup on his stomach. "But that is brilliant news, detective. Let me guess, Becs?"

As he weighed up his response, Garrick noticed a new copy of Flying Magazine was open on the classifieds section. "Tell me about you and Huw Crawford."

Fraser's brow furrowed. "Crawford... Crawford... you'll have to give me more to go on."

"He's in a relationship with Terri."

Fraser leaned forward in his seat, resting his arms on his knees. He knocked the coffee back in one gulp and put the cup on the table.

"I knew she was seeing some other fella. But it's not really my business. Why him?"

Garrick was disappointed to see that Fraser looked as confused as he was feeling.

"He ran over a police officer while resisting arrest. He recognised me from your hotel room. He was the one trying to rob you. He was also involved with a security truck heist in Tonbridge a couple of weeks ago, with an old friend of yours. Oscar Benjamin."

All signs of ease vanished from Fraser. His right knee began to nervously judder.

"He's no friend of mine, I can assure you. Although I think the worst revenge that I could unleash on him is to encourage him to stay with Becs. What makes you say he and Crawford did this thing?"

"He used the same gun in the heist and to rob you."

Fraser gave a dry chuckle and shook his head in disbelief. "Some people..."

"It appears that Crawford was dragged into this through his girlfriend. Terri. Speaking of who..." Garrick gestured to the two new paintings he had noticed when he entered. He instantly recognised them as Hoys: large and awful. "Another two new Hoys?"

"You're keeping me other two in evidence." Fraser stood and moved closer to one to admire it. "I see you're developing quite an eye."

"Let's just say I know what I like." Garrick hadn't meant to sound so disparaging. "And I know Terri is your mysterious artist. Don't worry. Your secret is safe with me. Unless of course she's implicated in this mess as anything other than a victim. In which case, I would start searching for a new golden goose."

Fraser didn't turn around. His fists clenched. Garrick had been hoping for more of a reaction, but in retrospect, he had potentially just destroyed Fraser's route to fame and fortune.

When he spoke again, Fraser's voice was barely above a whisper. "Terri is an innocent in this. She's too trusting. Too naïve."

"Are you saying that as the father of her child, or...?"

Fraser sharply turned with a thunderous expression. "He is not mine. How many paternity tests do I need to take? It doesn't matter what she says. It doesn't alter the truth that she slept around."

"Which is what you were doing too, between her and your wife. And you suspected she and Mark were sleeping together."

"She was sleeping with everyone behind me back." He drew in a sharp breath to calm himself. "But that has nothing to do with anything. This Crawford fella is after our time together. Terri has nothing to gain from doing me in. Rebecca, on the other hand..."

"She potentially gets her hands on the house and a valuable artist. And Mark?"

Fraser became pensive as he turned back to the art. "He was just in the way, wasn't he? Poor sod."

"He was also using the gallery to launder money."

Fraser searched for something to say. "He was always looking for a get-rich-quick scheme."

"Aren't we all? And he knew Oscar Benjamin through you."

"I would hardly say they were friends." He held up a hand. "And before you ask one of your meandering questions, I did my time – which I still say was a miscarriage of justice."

"Naturally."

"And I had no jiggery-pokery involving Mark. I wouldn't have even suggested something illegal to him. Or to anyone," he quickly added. "I'm a bona fide member of the art community these days." He lifted his chin, daring Garrick to challenge him.

"So I see." Garrick stood, a jolt of electricity shooting through his backside. He hadn't told the paramedics about his wing mirror spanking and was now wondering if something was fractured. He looked at the paintings. Fraser caught his look.

"You still don't see, do you?"

"I think these are worse than the last two."

"That's because people inherently try to bring people who are more successful than themselves down. There's a famous saying about it: *everybody's a critic.*"

25

"You're certain that you've had no interaction with Huw Crawford?" asked Detective Sergeant Okon, as Garrick poured a paper cup of water for Rebecca. Rebecca took the cup and sipped it, then shook her head. Out of habit, Garrick checked the video was recording her every expression.

"You've asked my client that three different times," said her solicitor, consulting his legal pad. "And each time she has replied the same way."

Garrick resisted a snide comment. He let Chib run the interview since the case was coming together so neatly. He was still in pain when he sat, but had fared far better than DC Harry Wilkes, who was being kept in hospital suffering a concussion, a dislocated left shoulder, and had broken his right leg in two places. Garrick was hoping he'd have time to pop into the hospital to see him before the end of the day, although he suspected that Rebecca wouldn't crack so quickly.

"I'm just trying to find out if she has remembered anything new," Chib replied with an easy smile.

In her cell, Rebecca Ellis had been unaware of the incident with Huw Crawford, but Garrick knew all too well that her solicitor's confidential discussion before the interview would have alerted her to developments. Crawford appeared to have pulled off a trick and was still hiding from the authorities despite the intensive manhunt and his face being plastered across the news thanks to Molly Meyers' enthusiastic reporting.

Chib laid the picture of Rebecca and the black-clad figure loading the bags into her boot.

"That is Terri Cordy." Chib leaned back in her chair and clasped her hands together. "By all means continue telling us about this phantom Jenny friend of yours. But Miss Cordy is now in custody. She's not as tight-lipped as you. Which probably shouldn't be a surprise since she has a child to consider in all of this. You're not a mother, are you? You don't know how strong that bond can be."

Rebecca glowered at Chib but said nothing. Garrick could almost feel the slap Chib's veiled threat contained. So far, all Terri Cordy had done was sob hysterically and answer only the most basic of questions. He made a mental note, Chibarameze Okon was not as sweet as she made out to be.

"Derek couldn't have children," Rebecca said quietly. "Thank God. It would've been like giving birth to a weasel." She took a moment to compose herself. "You have the wrong opinion about me."

"I can only form an opinion based on what you tell me, Rebecca." Chib's tone was warm. She was playing a one-woman good-cop/bad-cop routine.

"Everything I told you about Jenny's situation was the truth. Except, Jenny is Terri." She toyed with the photograph. "She wanted to get away from Huw. He was abusive. The problem is, she couldn't admit that to anybody. She certainly wouldn't admit that to you. But she was frightened and wanted to run." She picked up the photograph and studied it. "She really wanted to jump on the train and head to the continent. But she didn't even possess a passport. I was trying to help her move some things out, so that when she left, she wouldn't lose everything."

They'd ran background checks on Huw Crawford. There was no sign of a violent past, he came across as the quiet boy next-door. However, the armed robbery, attack on Fraser, and the hit-and-run were more than enough to convince Garrick that Crawford was a nasty piece of work.

Rebecca shifted in her seat, battling her own self-doubt. Garrick was surprised to see tears roll down her cheeks. Just how good an actress was she?

"The plan was for me to move as many of her things as I could to Portugal. She was going to stay with Oscar and me until she could find her feet."

Garrick couldn't hold back. "That was very understanding of you."

She fixed him with her steely gaze. "You do not know how understanding I am, Detective." She spat the words out as if they were a threat.

"Once she has her passport, she's coming over with little Ethan."

"It sounds like you spent a lot of time planning it," said Chib softly. "Which is confusing because you told us you'd only come over when you discovered Derek was still alive."

"Oscar had suggested it before all of this happened." She waved her hand to take in the interview room. "And I came to see for myself that the son of a bitch was still alive, and to find Oscar."

"Oh, we're still looking," Garrick said. "Don't worry about that. In fact, Interpol has just issued a Red Notice for him. Do you know what a Red Notice means?"

Rebecca gave a thin smile. "It means he can be arrested and brought back here for questioning. I also know what it isn't. It *isn't* an international arrest warrant. Which means you are scrambling to find any evidence to link him to your *theories*."

She was irritating Garrick more than usual. Mainly because she was right, but partly because his migraine was returning. They had evidence that placed Crawford at the heist, and assaulting Fraser and Garrick at the hotel, but nothing yet that placed him with the corpse in Fraser's house or the death of Mark Kline-Watson, other than the ownership of the gun.

"If you ask me, Rebecca, it looks as if your beloved Oscar Benjamin has disappeared so you can all take the fall for everything he's done. Just like his brother did."

"For what he's done? Enlighten me."

Garrick held up the Tonbridge Station car park photo. "You met Terri Cordy here. She came straight from London. We have her movements logged on the tube gates, she swiped in and out of. You didn't meet to help her move her possessions out because she had very few of them to begin with. I saw her flat. In fact, according to the CCTV footage, she arrived empty-handed. Those bags were ones you picked up from Stanley Matthews' dealership next door. You must know good old Stan. He's an old friend of your beloved Oscar."

He noted the solicitor's growing concern. Obviously, the facts were not tallying with what she'd told him.

"Those bags were then spirited away."

Rebecca leaned back in her chair and crossed her legs. She kept one hand on the table, tracing lazy patterns across the surface.

"Why would we do that?"

"One thing about the heist that puzzled me, although it was smart. Risky, but smart. They performed the getaway on foot. No car to be stopped and swabbed for forensic evidence. Just a quick sprint down a couple of streets and they can deposit the bags at good old Stanley Matthews' dodgy dealership and stroll out of town looking like a pair of innocent blokes. Then, after they lie low and things die down, they can send in their better halves to pick up the loot."

The intrepid solicitor waved his pen to intervene. "I'm sorry, but this isn't right. You arrested my client on suspicion over the death of Mark Kline-Watson and the other fellow in Mr Fraser's house. Yet you are now trying to connect her to an armed robbery that happened when she was out of the country? Are there any other unsolved crimes the Kent constabulary wants to throw at her? This is ridiculous! I demand that you release her immediately!"

Garrick completely blanked the indignant man. "That cash was bound for Mark Kline-Watson, wasn't it? Terri introduced Fraser to him. Fraser introduced Oscar when you were still married and having an affair. At the time, Mark was using his second-hand shop in Islington as a front to launder money. His gallery in Rye was supposed to carry that on and maybe shift more money. Except he wasn't really selling very much until Hoy's artwork appeared on the scene. Now moving around larger sums of cash would be a lot easier. But what if Mark suddenly decided not to play ball? Or perhaps demand a larger cut? It's the sort of thing that could lead to arguments, or even..." he let the word *murder* hang in the air.

Rebecca stared wide-eyed at him for several long moments.

Then she burst into laughter. She was laughing so hard that tears trickled down her face.

"Oh my God!" She exclaimed. "That's amazing. I mean, you have those bags, right? You have the loot all neatly bundled up inside?" She wiped the tears away with the back of her hand. Her frivolity suddenly turned into deep menace. "When I walk out of here, I can't wait to find out how many other innocent people you've harassed and nicked, because the media tempest that's going to be generated will hurt you, Detective."

Her solicitor was now incandescent. "Just to be clear, Detectives. You don't have this alleged money. Or the bags. Or witnesses, or evidence that place my client and Mr Crawford together. Or, indeed, place her at the scene of Mr Kline-Watson's murder, other than she was seen earlier that day demanding to know where her partner was. That has been her crime – caring about the man she loves. Nothing more."

The rest of the interview went downhill from there.

HARRY LORD WAS SITTING up in his bed when Garrick entered the private room. His leg was in plaster and the bandage around his head looked almost comical. His arm was held in a plastic sling, but despite it all, he was grinning.

"You're not the only one who can make it on the news!" he cried with pride. "Have you seen it?"

"I was there, mate."

"Some students filmed it all on their phones. Wham! I went over that car like the Six Million Dollar Man!"

Garrick forced a laugh. His encounter with Rebecca had dampened his spirits more than he could even admit to Chib. His migraine reached such intensity that during the drive to the hospital, the headlights from oncoming traffic felt like needles stabbing his eyeballs.

"Except they rebuilt Steve Austin as a state-of-the-art robot," he said, recalling the vaguest childhood TV memories. "The best we can do for you is a bit of Lego."

"Well, the wife loves it. You just missed her. I tell you what, if you ever need your love life spicing up, just get hit by a car."

"Your relationship advice is second to none. At least the students knew how to use their phones. None of them wanted to try out CPR." He raised a plastic bag he was carrying. "I bought you a get-well-soon prezzie. Something I know you'll find useful."

Harry eagerly snatched the bag and opened it as Garrick sat on the chair by the side of his bed and plucked a few grapes from the obligatory fruit Harry's wife had left behind.

"Oh. Brilliant." Harry raised the bicycle crash helmet Garrick had bought from Halfords on his way down. Harry pretended to throw it at Garrick and both men howled with laughter.

Garrick looked around the Kent and Canterbury Hospital room. "Not a bad room this one."

"Yeah. I think it's the only one down here I haven't spent a night in." Harry's career had seen him collect several injuries, including a minor stab wound. But this latest one had taken first place in his injury leader board. His voice dropped in horror. "You don't think they let any of those students prac-tise here, do you?"

"I think that's a distinct possibility. As Crawford burned off with you on his bonnet, all I could see was his *'I love K+C'* bumper sticker."

Harry raised the sheet and glanced at his crotch. "I'm amazed they haven't accidentally snipped my balls off then."

"Don't worry," Garrick assured him. "They do micro-surgery at a completely different university."

Harry plucked a grape and threw it at Garrick's head. "You're a bastard, sir."

"Privilege of rank."

"You got him yet?" Harry said, suddenly sober.

Garrick shook his head. "He's a rat alright. Gone to ground, but we'll collar him," he added with optimism he didn't feel.

Harry became reflective. "He was really bloody fright-ened. I saw his face, right until I nutted the windshield. Wide eyes. Petrified."

Just as he had been at the hotel, thought Garrick.

He told him about Rebecca Ellis's scathing rebuttal. He had to admit, some parts were tenuous, but the main thrust of her allegations felt right. Or at least they didn't feel wildly wrong. He recalled Drury's warning about Rebecca being the type who peppered lies with just enough truths.

Terri Cordy had been uncooperative since coming down from London. He had intended to interview her next, but after the shambles with Rebecca, all Garrick wanted to do was sleep and approach things with new zeal in the morning. He was still convinced that, in the absence of Oscar Benjamin, Huw Crawford would unlock everything.

He told Harry about how Rebecca had responded when he revealed Hoy's identity.

"She doesn't believe it's Terri?"

"She found the very idea laughable. Said she might've studied art in uni, but she had no skills. The Met arrested her and searched the flat. They found some paints, brushes and a couple of small canvases."

He showed the photographs they had sent through. Two depicted bowls of fruit and another of her sleeping baby.

"These were watercolours. Hoy's stuff is oil on canvas. The second issue is obvious."

Harry scrolled through the pictures, then nodded. "She's bloody good."

They may not be professional quality, but at least they were not the abstract mess Fraser's peddling.

Harry passed the phone back. "You've got a message. Didn't you say Fraser confirmed she was our missing artist?"

Garrick had silenced the phone on entering the hospital and had missed the call from Chib. He dialled his voicemail as he recalled Fraser's reaction.

"He just sort of went with it. He didn't actually say..." He fell silent as he listened to the short message. Then he hung up and stared at the screen.

"I suppose if we have nothing to charge her with then Rebecca's out tomorrow?" When Garrick didn't answer, Harry turned to him and saw the shocked look on his face. "What's happened?"

"They just found Huw Crawford."

26

H uw Crawford's body swung in the cold wind blowing in from the North Sea, heralding the storm that was poised to hit Whitstable. He was at the top of a thirty-foot tall metal tower that held a raft of weather monitoring devices. It was accessible by a steel-rung ladder, which is how Crawford had got all the way to the top, carrying a length of rope left amongst the building supplies dumped between the popular seafood shacks. He'd fastened one end of the rope to the rungs, the other around his neck. Every so often the wind would pick up, causing the body to swing wide and clang Crawford's Timberland boots against the mast. It was the very noise that had attracted a pair of diners to look up as they headed to their car.

If it wasn't for the wind, the body could have gone unnoticed all night at the top of the pole, wreathed in darkness. By the time Garrick had arrived, the police at the scene had rigged a pair of spotlights to illuminate him.

Garrick's first instinct was to cut him down, but that proved tricky. Simply slashing the rope would send the body crashing to the ground and destroy vital evidence. It was another two hours before the SOCO team arrived, just as the rain squall moved in. They eventually called in a scissor lift so they could retrieve the body.

It was well after midnight when a uniformed officer knocked on the side window of Garrick's Land Rover, causing him to jump. He'd been fending off sleep since he took refuge in his car while the forensics did their thing. The officer led him to the foot of the weather mast. A middle-aged SOCO pulled her rain poncho tighter. He recognised her from a few other past crime scenes, which was made easier with her Australian accent. She had to shout over the noise of the rain hammering the metal roofs of the diners and small warehouses around them.

"I can't be sure, but I think he's been dead for about three hours. If it wasn't for the wind bashing him against the mast, I don't think anybody would've found him until the morning." She had to raise her voice as the rain pelted harder. It stung Garrick's eyes every time he followed her finger up to the mast. His hair was plastered to his scalp. His legs were wet, feet soaked, and the water had trickled down the neck of his Barbour, drenching his shirt. "I think it's odds-on-favourite it was a suicide. Getting a body way up there to fake it would be far too difficult."

She crossed to a pallet filled with building materials and some junk. "I reckon he got the rope from here. So unless he specifically intended to come to this place, it wasn't premeditated."

This was the desperate act of a frightened man. The hit-and-run had been all over the news, so it was no secret that DC Lord had survived. He doubted it was the guilt of the incident that had led Huw to take his own life. They were only two miles from where Crawford had dumped the car, so he must have spent several hours hiding in Whitstable before making his fatal decision.

"What did he have on him?"

"Nothing. But we found this bag in one of the dumpsters." She pointed to a line of wheel refuge bins that had all been tipped onto their sides so the team could examine their contents. She led him to the back of a forensic van. They both climbed inside, thankful to be out of the storm. The rain drummed the vehicle as she swapped her blue latex gloves for a pair of dry ones and then laid a leather satchel on a sheet on the floor. She carefully drew out a laptop, a medical textbook, and a mobile phone.

Garrick took a pair of latex gloves from a cardboard box and put them on. He opened the laptop. It woke from sleep, showing a password prompt.

"That's gonna be fun to hack," sniffed the SOCO.

Garrick tried to access the phone. That too was locked.

"Is the body still here?"

"In the Ambulance."

Garrick braced himself as he hopped from the van and ran to the back of the ambulance into which the body had been loaded. He held up the phone so its camera could scan Huw Crawford's face. It failed to unlock. Garrick tried again. It didn't work. He'd tried a similar trick with Fanta in the past, and it had worked perfectly.

The SOCO caught up with him and clambered onboard.

"I don't think this is his phone," sighed Garrick.

"It probably has the attention feature switched on." Garrick's bewildered expression made her chuckle. "I wouldn't have known about it if my daughter hadn't slipped up and told me. So nobody can unlock your phone while you're asleep, the software checks to see if you're awake."

She leaned across the body and used both hands to pry Crawford's eyelids open. His bulging glassy eyes stared at an angle, but the pupils were just visible.

"Try it now."

Garrick held up the camera and the screen unlocked. He went straight into the settings and turned the phone's auto-lock off. It was another handy tip that Fanta had taught him. He checked the call log and saw twenty-three calls to the same number. A quick check on his own phone confirmed it was Terri Cordy's mobile. Over the space of several hours, right until nine-sixteen, they had gone unanswered. The only other call was to an unregistered mobile made five minutes after Crawford had struck officer Lord. It lasted for three-minutes four-seconds.

A quick check of his emails, text messages, Facebook, and WhatsApp revealed no new activity for the last couple of days.

Garrick's head was literally spinning. He made a note of the unregistered mobile number and emailed Fanta to check it out as soon as she reached the incident room in the morning. He handed the phone back to the SOCO, thanked the team for their efforts, and squelched back to his car.

He turned the radio on and blasted nineties dance tunes from KMFM just to keep him awake. It didn't quite work as the repetitive beats of Snap's '*Rhythm is a Dancer*' lulled him. His mind kept circling the anomalies scattered amongst the evidence.

While there were plenty of connections between the various players and a snarl of motivation, animosity, and bitter romance, none of them linked in the right way. He had been relying on Crawford to provide him with that spark of final inspiration, but now that had been snatched from him.

Back home, Garrick threw his damp clothes into the bathtub and, naked, collapsed under the bedsheets. He sank into a brooding series of dreams in which he was being pursued while his sister constantly attempted to warn him of *something*, but the words were never clear and, at times, sounded backwards.

He woke in the morning feeling even more tired than he had at the start of the night.

AN EMAIL from DC Liu confirmed that the three-minute phone call Crawford had made was to an unregistered pay-as-you-go phone. Garrick made the decision that a grief counsellor should break the news of Crawford's death to Terri before they interviewed her. That was one session he was not looking forward to today, and one that he couldn't, as a leader, throw to Chib to deal with. Although she'd be much better at handling it than him.

He had a sparky email from Wendy, which painfully reminded him they hadn't talked since *that night* in Pizza Hut. What must she think of him? He promised to call her at lunchtime before she thought he was being stand-offish.

Overnight, a polite refusal to hand over any information had arrived from Fraser's bank in Panama. Garrick was just finishing his breakfast when he received an irate call from Dr Rajasekar.

"You missed your appointment!" she snapped with no preamble.

"I didn't think we had an appointment booked."

"For your MRI!"

Garrick's stomach jolted. "I completely forgot. Wait, I thought it was the end of the week? I remember you saying it was the end of the week."

"No, David. I spoke to you yesterday and said it was first thing this morning. An hour ago! They called me to ask where you were."

With everything that had happened, Garrick was getting confused. He remembered her exact words, or perhaps he'd been distracted.

"To be honest, I had to pull a few strings to get you that." Rajasekar was determined to make him feel bad. "This is your health we're talking about. You must take it seriously."

"I do." He sounded like a chastised schoolboy.

"As luck would have it, they've had another cancellation this morning and juggled appointments around for you. Get to Tunbridge Wells for ten-fifteen. Same place as last time."

The words '*I can't*' caught in his throat. He glanced at the time; it was eight-thirty. By the time he got to the station, he would have to perform a U-turn and go straight to the hospital, so it wasn't worth going to the office. He mumbled an apology and his thanks before assuring her he'd be there on time. Then he hung up and called Chib who was at her desk and catching up with the overnight events. Now it really looked as if he was throwing her under the bus as he asked her to interview Terri Cordy. Although, if she thought that, she never let on.

"We're releasing Rebecca in the next hour. We're just waiting for her solicitor to turn up. Should we be following her?"

"The way things are going, that will not make us look good if she finds out. Let's make sure Border Force alert us when she tries to leave."

He filled her in on retrieving Huw Crawford's body. She'd read the incident report, but Garrick's account added a missing layer of tragedy.

"I don't get it," said Chib. "He was a good-looking bloke. A medical student with great grades. Why would he jeopardise any of that?"

"The corny answer is what drives anybody to do extreme things: love."

After finishing his call, he realised he had a good fifty minutes on his hands before he had to leave. He made himself a matcha tea and sat in front of his ammonite. He hated the MRI, so tackling the finer details of his fossil with a small metal brush proved to be a relaxing distraction.

He alternately sipped his tea and used the mounted magnifying glass to peer closer into the ridges of the shell. Apart from the ridges he'd accidentally shaved away, the rest of the detail was rather magnificent. Mounted on a base of the rock he found it in, it would look quite handsome on the mantlepiece. He felt proud. Impulsively, he powered up the air pump and use the air scribe to cut away a little more of the base to give it shape. The scribe's tiny needle chipped effortlessly through the rock, but the shrill whine of the pump triggered another pounding headache. Surely this had to be psychosomatic, he thought. It was a question to pose to Dr Rajasekar. He was distracted. Too distracted.

A chunk of matrix the size of a two-pound coin suddenly fell away. There had been a crack in the rock he hadn't noticed. As the base material crumbled, the beautiful ammonite fractured in two.

Garrick stopped the pump and angrily tossed the air scribe aside. He picked up the two halves. They neatly fitted together, so he could glue them, but that would be cheating.

He was annoyed. A month's diligent work had been suddenly ruined on an impulse. Disgusted with himself, he threw the two parts onto his wooden workboard.

Then he noticed there was something *inside* the ammonite. Curious, he flipped it over. No, not inside. It was a claw or a tooth that had cracked the once-living mollusc open from behind. The last act of a predator before something had killed it too, eventually leaving only their fossilised remains. Garrick took heart that predator's crime had eventually come to light millennia later...

THE FEELING of being entombed in the MRI scanner was worse than last few times. The experience was further compounded by the machine's rhythmic, heavy thumping as it scanned the inside of his skull. Each sound sent his migraine pulsing, and he wondered if that would show on the scan.

While waiting to go in, he'd scrolled through his phone and found his original appointment was in his calendar, put there yesterday by himself when Rajasekar had called. Yet he distinctly recalled her telling him it was at the end of the week. He remembered every word of the message. He recalled the sinking feeling of having to go through the whole experience again. Was he so tired he was getting easily confused? Had he latched onto a false memory and convinced himself it was real? Either way, it alarmed him. And he wasn't completely sure he should mention it to Rajasekar during their next session.

He was in and out in thirty minutes, knowing the results would land with his doctor soon. He only hoped that it would be good news.

27

H e arrived at the station to discover Chib still hadn't interviewed Terri Cordy as she'd broken down when told about Huw Crawford's death. She was only able to talk a few hours later, so Garrick hadn't escaped the ordeal after all. Her eyes were bloodshot, but her voice was quiet but firm. He was surprised to find her so remarkably composed.

"Huw and I were no longer dating."

Garrick nodded in understanding. "How long have you been apart?"

"Well, we were never really an item." She flushed and kept scratching her nose, embarrassed about discussing her personal life. "It was more off than on."

"When did you last see him?"

She exhaled a long sigh as she thought. "Two months? Maybe more. He called me a lot. I got annoyed. Told him not to. He wouldn't leave me alone."

"And how did he react to that?"

"He was very upset."

"Aggressive? Argumentative?"

She gave a snort. "Huw was always argumentative. But never violent."

Garrick mentally logged Rebecca Ellis's lie.

"I'm curious about why Huw might have a grudge against Derek."

"Where to begin? Derek has a talent for rubbing people up the wrong way."

"Anything specific?" Chib asked with a tinge of hostility that surprised Garrick. She clearly wasn't buying into Terri's suddenly calm and vulnerable persona.

"Derek and I had a real relationship. Something Huw couldn't have." Was it Garrick's imagination or did she sneer?

"But you and Derek split up because of the baby."

"He left me! I wanted us to stay together, but *he* left *me*! We could've worked things out if only he'd given it a chance."

"Your affair led to his divorce."

"That was on the cards anyway. Those two mutually loathed each other from the beginning. God knows why they got ever married."

"You must've hated Rebecca Ellis for taking him back from you."

"No. It wasn't her fault. The only reason he tried to patch things up with her was because it would ruin him financially if they split."

"Because she would take half his possessions. The liquid ones. Leaving him with nothing."

"That's more than he deserved." She folded her arms and grimaced at the memory.

Garrick was confused. "I thought you were in love with him?"

"Not after he chucked me away. I was naïve then. I'm not

now. When I heard that he'd died, I was glad. It actually made me miss Huw."

Garrick drummed his fingers on the table, taking some pleasure to see it was irritating her.

"Back to why Huw would break into Derek's hotel room and threaten him with a gun to steal some valuable artwork."

She frowned. "What?"

"Come on. You can't be the only person who didn't see him make a fool of me on the television news."

"I saw that. But it was Huw?"

"You didn't recognise him?"

"Are you serious? It was too blurry and shaky. I didn't even recognise you. Huw wouldn't have done that."

"Maybe he did it to impress you?" Chib suggested.

"And how would that impress me? No. I don't believe he would do that."

Garrick pursed his lips. "For the sake of argument, suppose he was trying to steal them to get a better deal with the art buyer, a man you happened to both know. A man who was perhaps using his business to launder money."

Terri nodded. "Mark. Typical."

"You knew about Mark's extracurricular activities?"

"Detective, please!" her solicitor cried out, speaking for the first time since he had arrived. "You're leading her."

"How else can I say it? Did you know he was a crook?"

She raised a hand dismissively. "I suspected it. But I didn't know it. I didn't want to get involved. I met Huw through him."

Chib made a note in her pad. "While in London?"

Terri nodded. "He was just folding up his shop in Islington and thinking of moving down south."

"And how did they know each other?"

"Huw tried to sell him a few pieces of his art."

Garrick was surprised. "He was an artist?"

"That's what we had in common. He was good, but I suppose he thought there was more money to be made being a doctor. We were friends, I suppose. He moved to Kent to study when Derek and I got together. I hardly saw him until Derek dumped me. He was a rebound thing."

Chib thoughtfully tapped her pen on the notepad. Garrick suspected she had just reached the same conclusion he had. He showed her the CCTV footage on his phone showing her and Rebecca placing the holdalls in the back of the Fiat.

"Talk us through what's happening here."

Terri studied it for a long moment. Then tossed it aside.

"They're my things. I told you I was moving. Rebecca is taking them to Portugal and as soon as I have my passport, Ethan and I will join her."

"That's a very generous thing for a woman like her to do, especially as her ex-husband had been sleeping with you. Why would she humour you now? She's a person you admit to not knowing very well."

Terri looked at Garrick as if he'd announced he was the Pope. "She's a nice person. But she's not doing it for me. She's doing it for Ethan's father."

Now it was Garrick's turn to look confused. "Derek?"

"*Oscar!*" She looked between Garrick and Chib. "Oscar is Ethan's father."

Garrick lolled back in his seat, scrambling to insert this new piece of knowledge into the puzzle. "You took a paternity test. You said Ethan was Derek's child."

"Of course I did. I loved Derek. Oscar was a stupid one-night stand. We were drunk. I was pissed off with Derek. It was before Oscar and Rebecca had got together, so she understands. Derek was always shooting blanks. As soon as he found out I was pregnant, he was delighted. But when he discovered the truth... he didn't want to know me. At least Oscar was a gentleman. And now he wants what's best for his son."

"And a new life for you."

Garrick had assumed that Rebecca's comment about Derek being unable to father children had been nothing more than spite, not biological fact.

Chib indicated the photo. "Where are the bags? They were not in Rebecca's Airbnb or her car. And you arrived from London without them. And an empty one was found in your apartment. Why would Stanley Matthews have your possessions?"

"Because Oscar had asked Stan to look after me. I don't have a car or storage. He has a whole dealership. That's where my boxes are going."

Garrick was once again feeling that his list of suspects was dwindling. Rebecca Ellis had been freed. They had nothing to hold Terri on, and it was all down to one man who had hanged himself.

WHILE CHIB DEALT with releasing Terri Cordy, Garrick stood in front of the evidence wall. The nameless corpse had to be linked to Huw Crawford in an attempt to impersonate Derek Fraser, a man he hated because of their love feud over Terri and the child. A child fathered by Oscar Benjamin. A man with a grudge against Fraser.

For whatever reason he couldn't fathom, the imperson-ation had gone wrong, so had the attempt at stealing the artwork been a desperate last-minute bid? Had Mark Kline-Watson – a man in need of the money - threatened to expose them, forcing Huw to silence him? Had Huw's actions been encouraged by Oscar Benjamin? Or an act of desperation because Oscar had really abandoned him, Terri, and Rebecca, taking the stolen cash with him?

And the security truck heist... Garrick was still mulling that. Was it simply a case of opportunity? Two separate crimes that were too tempting for the same crooks.

Then there was the possibility that Huw was the mysterious Hoy...

The harsh sound of coins jangling in a cup close to his ear broke him from his reverie. Fanta was holding a mug sporting the Kent Police crest. She shook it again. By the sound of it, there was only a bit of loose change inside.

"I'm collecting for Harry!" She shoved the mug under Garrick's nose.

"Why? He's getting sick pay."

Fanta's eyes widened in protest. "Sir! That's a horrible thing to say. He was injured in the line of duty!"

Garrick felt the pain in his buttock twinge. That made two of them.

"As our commanding officer, you're expected to set the bar high. Not tight."

"Oh, really? How much did Superintendent Drury contribute?"

Fanta sheepishly lowered the cup. "I wanted her to be awed by the rest of the team's generosity."

Garrick angled the cup down and counted the contents. "One-pound-forty? What treasures are you planning to buy him?"

"I've just started."

Garrick took his wallet from his pocket and pulled out his debit card. "Where should I swipe this?"

Fanta glowered at him and slammed the cup on a table near the evidence board. "I shall leave this here so everybody can make a donation."

Garrick put his card away. "How about doing something really useful? Terri Cordy claims that her baby's father is Oscar Benjamin, not Fraser. Fraser took a paternity test. See what's on file."

Eighty minutes later, she returned with the news that Rebecca Ellis had just checked in at Gatwick Airport. She was leaving in a hurry.

She also had not one, but two shocking answers to Garrick's query.

And like that, the entire case cracked open, revealing the predator within.

28

"Nobody has come in, and he hasn't left," said the bored officer sitting in the patrol car at the end of Fraser's drive.

As Garrick and Chib approached, they could see him playing a game on his phone. The copper flinched when they knocked on his window, so his observational skills were questionable.

"When was the last time you saw him?" Garrick noticed there was a small mailbox bolted onto the wall just outside the gate.

"About an hour ago he came out and offered me a cuppa. He's been good at doing that for everyone."

"And he's had no visitors?" The copper shook his head.

Chib followed Garrick up the driveway. The living room lights were on, but all seemed quiet. She rang the bell as Garrick peered through the windows. The curtains were drawn.

"Maybe he's asleep?" Chib said after thumbing the doorbell for the third time.

Garrick motioned for her to follow him to the plyboard covering the broken patio window. He wedged his fingers against the lip of a vertical slat and heaved. Only when he put his full bodyweight into it did the wood give as nails pried free.

"What're you doing?"

"I'm concerned that he could be on the floor, bleeding to death!"

He heaved again. The wood cracked so loudly that they were both surprised when the cop on guard duty didn't come running. Garrick rested the freed six-foot wooden panel against the other door, then he stepped into the extension.

Nothing had changed. Even the two Hoy paintings were on the wall.

"Derek?" He yelled. "It's DCI Garrick!"

No answer.

The square of carpet still hadn't been replaced. He moved into the kitchen, noticing the lights had been left on.

"Derek?"

"I'll check upstairs," said Chib.

She hurried off before Garrick could caution her that it might be dangerous. He realised how bad that could sound in this day and age. He was sure Chib was more than proficient in self-defence, maybe more so than he was. He had trained on the streets, in the art of gouging and punching when your opponent wasn't looking.

He tried the backdoor. Locked. From above came the sounds of Chib dashing from room-to-room, and he could just hear her calling for Fraser.

The kitchen counters were tidy, the sink empty. Garrick leaned against a cupboard as he took in the room, searching for anything amiss. He dialled Fraser's mobile – and it rang in the kitchen. Fraser found it just behind the fruit bowl. He heard Chib hurry down the stairs and check the dining room. Then she reappeared in the kitchen.

"He's not here."

"He's left his mobile." Garrick looked back at the empty sink. He sniffed the air. There was a strong lingering smell. He turned his head in a slow circle, tracing the odour under the sink. He gingerly opened the cupboard.

Inside was a bottle of bleach, window cleaner, a packet of dishwasher tablets, and a bottle of turps. The dishwasher was alongside the cupboard, its wooden facade neatly blending it with the other work units. He opened it. Inside were a few cups, plates, and placed neatly upright amongst the cutlery: four paint brushes. He took one out and held it up so Chib could see.

"It seems we have a keen artist." He indicated under the sink. "Turpentine to clean them. He's been using oil paints."

Chib's eyes widened. "Fraser is Hoy?"

"That's why he wasn't in a rush to disabuse me of my idea about it being Terri."

They walked into the living room, searching for fresh clues. Garrick looked down at the hole in the carpet, recalling the body lying there.

The man who looked like Fraser.

No. Not entirely. The watch imprint on the wrist. The coroner said it had been too tight for comfort. The clothes that were not quite the right cut. He'd been dressed to look like Fraser just before his murder. Then there was the paternity result.

Fraser had said the baby wasn't his. He had been correct. He and Terri knew it was Oscar Benjamin's. The paternity test confirmed that. Except the DNA taken for the test also matched that of the victim found on Fraser's floor.

It was Oscar Benjamin.

The two men had been roughly the same size. Fraser was prematurely white-haired, while Oscar was blond, hence the victim's dyed hair. Side-by-side they looked nothing alike, but with a smashed-up face...

Garrick moved into the hallway. There was an empty coat peg and the rack of shoes under the stairs seemed to be missing a pair.

"Fraser's done a runner," he said.

He was about to return to the living room when he spotted the pair of new green wellies stashed behind the shoes. Nothing unusual about that, except he couldn't picture Fraser as the type to wear them. He doubted Fraser did his own gardening. He picked them up and examined the sole. Something glinted in the deep grooves. It was a single shard of broken glass.

Garrick hurried back into the living room, imagining the crime scene. He pointed to the broken door.

"Oscar Benjamin was already here. Beaten so badly that he was almost dead. Fraser broke the door himself to make it look like forced entry." He saw Chib's curious look. "There is a piece of glass in the wellies back there. Same sort that littered the carpet when I arrived. Forensics would've cleared every single shard by the time we let Fraser back in the house. So it shouldn't be there."

He stood at the end of the table and turned his hand into the shape of a gun, miming shooting the man. "Fraser kills him. The TV was on loud, to mask the gunshots. Then he leaves for the retreat, his alibi. He doesn't take his own car because people might see him leaving. I bet there's a gap in the garden fence that he can slip in and out of."

"Which is why the bloke at the gate hasn't seen him leave."

"He walks to the station... no," he corrected himself. "He's got to have been seen to have left earlier. He would've bought the train tickets to get him to Hay as a false trail, but somebody drove him there later."

"Rebecca?"

Garrick shook his head. "My money's on Huw Crawford."

Chib reacted with surprise. "Fraser checked into the hotel under fake name..."

"And kept himself to himself..."

"Until he left. Then he made a scene. Shouted a lot."

"So that people would remember he was there and reinforce his alibi. He'd left here with the intention of never coming back." He pointed to where the body had lain. "Oscar Benjamin was dressed like him and with his face smashed up nobody would know the difference. He'd even dyed his hair to be the same."

"And finding a dead man in his own house..."

"We wouldn't waste time doing a DNA analysis of the body. We just assumed. If he hadn't come back, then he could have got away with it." Garrick paced as he laid out the timeline. "Nobody came and found the body. He had no friends. There's a regular mailbox at the gate, so the postman wouldn't come this far, so there was little risk the body would be found until he wanted it to be."

"Which is why he ordered an Amazon package!"

"The body is discovered conveniently when he has been at the hotel for a day. The poor delivery guy, hearing the noise from the TV, seeing the broken window, stumbles over the body. The TV wasn't to mask the gunshots, it was to draw attention to the murder. The delivery guy calls the police. By which time the swelling and bruising on Oscar's face has become worse, making identification difficult."

"And how is Crawford tied into this?"

"The pathologist said that the broken jaw, teeth and cheekbones were done with just a little too much precision."

"Which a medical student would know."

"Huw either did it or advised Fraser. Just enough to make it look like torture, and just enough to leave Oscar Benjamin unrecognisable."

"But what brings Fraser back from the dead? Why go to all the effort of faking his own death using a man he hates?"

Garrick steepled both hands over his nose and mouth as he took in the scene once more. He started chuckling as tiny clues took on a whole new meaning.

"He was killing himself off and at the same time getting revenge on Oscar. Fraser was never coming back. He was hiding out in Hay – until the news of his death hit. That's what triggered the sudden interest in the Hoys he'd been trying to sell."

"His own work."

"Which he had tried to pass off as a new discovery. And it was working, just not enough."

"Until he died. And the price shot through the roof. Which would have left Mark Kline-Watson with his commission and Fraser's unclaimed share."

"So he makes a lot of noise at the Hotel in Hay so everybody can say he's been there the whole time. And he comes back. Makes a dramatic entrance..."

"And the value of the art keeps increasing as he magically produces more Hoys for sale." She nodded. "Right."

"Right."

"But…"

"You're going to find a hole in my theory, aren't you?"

"Only one I can drive a car through. Okay, maybe two. Why? He's running from creditors; he could just go missing without having to kill anybody. Especially not Oscar Benjamin. And Huw Crawford tried to rob him, not help him."

"You're wrong, Chib. You can drive a bus through it…" then a thought struck him. "Crawford and Mark Kline-Watson knew one another. Fraser and K-W were already in cahoots trying to sell the artwork… no, that doesn't make sense either…" Garrick slumped onto the sofa, his mind hopping from one random fact to another, desperate to draw them together.

"Although…" teased Chib. "What if we've been looking at this from completely the wrong end? You just said yourself that he came back from the dead because his art sold."

"Right."

"That was an unforeseen benefit. A side effect of his apparent death. Oscar Benjamin was over here two weeks before all of this, not to scam Fraser over an artist who was selling paintings for hardly anything. We know he came over for one last job. The security heist. Remember what Sean said, nobody wanted to work Oscar him after he let Noel take the fall. If he'd do that to his own brother… He needed somebody he could trust – not necessarily like – somebody who was as desperate as he was for the cash."

"Fraser? So it wasn't Crawford and Oscar holding up the truck. It was Fraser and Oscar…"

Chib nodded. "Fraser used the Colt he had got from Mark Kline-Watson."

Garrick stood suddenly as inspiration struck. "The same gun he then gave to Crawford. That's why he was using blanks, it was a stunt to drive up the price again." Garrick looked to the heavens as if it had been obvious. "Fraser wasn't drunk. His bar bill showed he'd bought hardly anything. He wanted Molly Meyer's there during the fake robbery, knowing it would be a huge press scoop."

"And he got you instead. And a video that went viral."

"Fraser was in the hotel the whole time. He could've cut the security cameras. And that's why Crawford looked so terrified when he saw me and tossed the gun as soon as he could. He knew Fraser's plan hadn't gone smoothly."

"Okay, I retract my statement. There's only one flaw. The money from the truck."

"The money from the heist wasn't what they had expected. Remember, there had been a last-minute change from the two million they'd been expecting. It wasn't enough to clear Fraser's debts. It wasn't enough to start Terri and Ethan up with a new life. They're going nowhere. And with Oscar out of the picture, Crawford thinks he can still win Terri back. Although he'd be living in fear of Fraser saying anything."

"And Mark Kline-Watson?"

"I don't think it was Rebecca or Terri. They may be a lot of things, but they're not killers. And I reckon one murder was enough for Crawford. Our favourite Scottish bastard has blood on his hands there."

"And now he's scarpered." Chib sighed in frustration. "He could be anywhere. What would you do if you were him?"

"Leave the country. But he's smart enough to know Border Force'll stop him." He shook his head. Then he spotted the new Flying magazine on the table.

"I think I know where he is!"

BRIDLE FARM WAS JUST over twenty minutes away outside the small village of Postling, and Fraser had a head start. With headlights still triggering his migraine, Garrick didn't trust himself to drive at speed, so he let Chib take the wheel of his Land Rover. She drove like a maniac, taking the blue light flickering on the dash as a sign to drive aggressively. Used to the instant power of her electric car, she was constantly grousing under her breath as Garrick's aging diesel failed to accelerate on demand, and the gears ground every time she shifted. She took the tight country bends at such reckless speeds that Garrick clung on to the door strap above his head to prevent him from being thrown out of his seat. As well as his headache, he now had to contend with severe motion sickness.

Following the GPS on his phone, they were soon racing down the narrow Pilgrim's Way. Their destination was up on the right.

The gate accessing the farm was wide open, and the huge farmhouse beyond was bathed in darkness. It was only 7pm and Garrick had recalled that the family were away.

Pulling onto the grounds, the headlights fell across a sign for Classic Aero, a renowned aircraft restoration company. Garrick had once listened enviously as one of his colleagues recounted a story of taking a ride here in their two-seater Spitfire. He'd always vowed to treat himself one day. A bucket list moment that he'd failed to achieve.

A dirt trail circled around the farmhouse, to an assortment of seven sheds and hangars at the back of the farm used for storing and repairing classic planes. The doors of two hangars were open and several small aircraft were just visible in the dark interior. Fraser's Mercedes was parked between the buildings.

Garrick lunged across the steering wheel. "Kill the headlights!" He found the switch and extinguished them. Chib cut the engine.

"That's his car," said Garrick. "He must have left it on the street so his protection wouldn't see him driving out."

As silently as they could, Garrick and Chib stepped out of the vehicle, leaving the doors ajar so as not to make any more noise. They stealthily approached the nearest hangar, keeping to the shadows and listening for any signs of which building Fraser had entered.

There was only the hoot of an owl from the fields beyond.

"Maybe he's gone already?" whispered Chib.

He had planned this, Garrick thought. He knew I was closing in, even if I didn't. He recalled that Huw Crawford tried to call Terri all night, but she didn't pick up. But he talked to somebody. Maybe a last damning accusation made to a burner phone before he took his own life. Shielding the glow of his mobile's screen, Garrick scrolled through the notes on his phone and found the number Huw Crawford had called. It rang–

And the classic Nokia *Grande Valse* echoed from the furthest hangar.

"There!" Garrick slipped the still-ringing phone in his pocket as he charged forward towards the noise.

Chib tried to follow, but her foot snagged on some junk in the shadows, and she fell flat on her face.

Garrick drew closer to the dark hangar – just as the growl of an engine drowned out the ringing phone. He could see nothing but darkness ahead. Then a huge shadow loomed, and he felt a sudden rush of air pulling him forward. At the last second, Garrick rolled aside as the whirling blades of a propellor slashed inches in front of his face.

He hit the ground hard. In the shadows, a wing sliced over his head. Garrick sprang to his feet and turned to see the silhouette of a biplane against the hangar doors. There was one figure sitting in the cockpit. The fool was going to fly himself out of the country.

Something suddenly struck him in the side, and Garrick felt a rib crack as he was pushed aside. He had forgotten about the tail's horizontal stabiliser. The breath was squeezed from him as he dropped to his knees, fighting the pain in his ribs.

A sudden steely determination pulsed through him, numbing the pain. He clambered to his feet, and on shaking legs, ran after the Boeing Stearman biplane. He almost cannoned into Chib at the entrance as the aircraft taxied between two sheds, heading out to a dark field.

"Get the car!" he snapped. Before she could reply, Garrick sprinted between a line of trees. He was gasping for breath as each step jarred his injured rib. He emerged on a long dark field. The ground was waterlogged, and cold mud seeped into his shoes. In the ambient light he could just see the shorter, paler grass which had been cut to form a basic unregulated runway. The aircraft was pointed away from him as the engine throttled up. There was no way he could stop it as it trundled forwards. He gave chase any way.

A blinding light came from his Land Rover's headlights as the vehicle suddenly sped onto the airstrip, cutting off the plane. The Stearman performed a tight U-turn as Fraser wrestled the rudder to avoid a collision. Now the aircraft was pointing straight at Garrick and still accelerating. Garrick didn't know if it was a deliberate assault, or if Fraser couldn't see him in the darkness. The manoeuvre was so sudden that Garrick skidded in the mud as he tried to stop.

He could barely breathe as the roaring biplane jounced towards him. He stopped, and then impulsively ran back the way he had come – but the aircraft was faster.

He was seconds away from being chewed up by the propellor.

The waterlogged airstrip was in no condition to take the weight of a plane. The wheels suddenly dug in the soft mud and the Stearman nosedived into the ground. The wooden propellors shattered on impact, leaving the engine howling. The biplane came to rest at an acute angle, tail-up, stranded in the field.

Garrick ran towards it as Fraser struggled to unfasten his belt. He motioned to clamber from the other side of the plane, intending to run, when Chib skidded the Land Rover to a halt, blocking his path.

"Derek Fraser," Garrick roared over the roar of the engine. "You're nicked, mate!"

29

Garrick glowered across the interview room. It was the following morning, and Fraser was crumpled over the table looking sorry for himself. Next to him, his solicitor, Rosamund Hellberg sat with a sullen look, knowing she was now backing a losing horse.

"I didn't see you in the dark," Fraser mumbled.

In Garrick's view, it was a poor excuse for attempted murder.

"And you could've run sideways," said Fraser sheepishly. "Who runs in a straight line?"

Despite the co-codamol Garrick had taken to combat his broken rib and piercing headache, he could still feel the pain. Between the bruises across his body, his sore buttocks, head, and rib, he was struggling to find an area that wasn't hurting.

Fraser was a defeated man. His arrogance was replaced by malaise. He had admitted to murdering Oscar Benjamin after they had both performed the security truck robbery.

"I was broke. I was going to lose everything, and the artwork wasn't selling for much. Aye, it was getting my face around and creating a bit of a mystery about this new talent, but I needed the cash now."

"So you screwed over your business partner?"

"Oscar only came to me to because he knew I wouldn't rat him out and nobody else trusted him. The deal was that he'd take seventy per cent to cover what I owed him." He shrugged as if it was self-explanatory. "We dumped the loot in Matthews' dealership and walked away. We didn't have time to count it. It was only when I saw the news that I realised we hadn't nabbed as much as expected. Eighty grand, not the two million we were expecting. So I broke in to steal it again. Not all of it, mind."

"No, you're too honest for that," Garrick muttered.

"Fifty grand. I thought it would look like Matthews was short-changing Oscar when we both turned up to claim it." He sighed and idly picked at the tabletop. "Huw helped me break in. He knew Oscar was going to use that cash to help Terri and Ethan leave the country to start a new life."

"Which you didn't want to happen."

Fraser looked incredulous. "Why would I want anything good to happen for that little cow? She slept with Oscar behind me back. Had his kid, which I originally thought was mine! After the paternity test showed it wasn't... that hurt."

He took a long gulp of water, emptying his paper cup. "I knew Huw would help because he didn't want her to go. Simple, right? I took the cash to Mark. I already had an offshore account lined up, and me and Oscar were going to use him to launder the loot, so it made sense. It made even more sense when we put the cash through the books to buy the Hoys we couldn't shift."

Garrick couldn't help but laugh. "Let me get this straight,

you used the now-twice stolen cash, to inflate the value of your own artwork?"

Fraser shrugged. "I didn't think it would make much of a difference. Mark got his commission; I got me money. I burnt the paintings," he added sadly.

"You could always whip a few more up in your kitchen, couldn't you?"

Fraser looked up in surprise. Then he smiled in utter defeat.

"Ah, well. That was a good ride while it lasted. Goes to show that I could've been a famous artist."

"If you hadn't killed anybody, then you could carry on painting like an infant, I suppose."

"Mark started demanding a bigger cut. I think he told Oscar what I did. I'm not sure, but Oscar confronted me." He lapsed into silence, replaying the memory. "I didn't mean to kill Oscar though It was an accident."

"But you didn't kill him, did you? He was still alive."

"It wasn't much of a difference, was it? When he came around, he'd kill me or have me killed. Oscar Benjamin was not a nice man. He was responsible for so many crimes he got away with while other people, like his own brother, did the time."

"And you thought that by killing him you'd be doing society a favour?" He had expected Hellberg to protest, but she remained quiet and disengaged.

"I thought many people, including me, would be better off without him. And I saw a chance of turning it all in. Starting anew."

"Faking your own death."

"Aye."

"Huw was training to be a doctor. He had aspirations of

being a plastic surgeon. He could've had quite the career. But you blackmailed him to use his knowledge and skill to disfigure Oscar Benjamin just enough that he could pass for you, under the right circumstances."

"I didn't think it would work that well. I thought it would buy me enough time to disappear." He smiled sadly and held up his hands. "Who would've thought my death would suddenly make Hoy a must have? That next piece sold for stupid money!"

"And with you dead, Mark Kline-Watson was under no obligation to pay you. So you had no choice but to come back from the dead."

Fraser waved both hands like a showman. "Ta-dah! Then guess what, I started making more money as Hoy than I could holding-up armoured cars."

"Inspiring. And the more you were in the news, the higher that price climbed."

"Exactly."

"That's why you persuaded Huw Crawford to fake an attempt on your life to steal the art, knowing that the reporter you'd been talking to was in the building at the same time."

"You got me."

"I don't think Huw did that willingly, did he?" Fraser looked away. "I bet you kept blackmailing him, didn't you? Told him how everybody would know about his involvement in killing Oscar. You laid on the guilt, knowing he'd buckle." Fraser stared at the table. At least he had the good grace to look regretful. Garrick was swelling with anger. "That's why he ran when he saw me. Knocking over DC Lord was an accident, but one that made his guilt and self-loathing push him to suicide. He felt he had no choice. You were blackmailing him. The woman he loved was still leaving the country. What else did he have? He killed himself. *Your* actions made him take his own life. *You* were the last person he called. What did he say to you?"

Fraser shook his head and refused to answer.

Garrick was struggling to keep the venom from his voice. "Because of that call, you knew I would turn up to ask you about the Terri connection. That gave you plenty of time to brew up an alibi. Didn't it? It's what made you decide to run last night. You've been playing everybody. You played me. Asking for protection, throwing accusations at everybody else to cover your own dirty tracks. Offering the cops assigned to protect you a cuppa and a biscuit, to lull them into a false sense of security so that you could park your car down the lane between shifts, ready to do a runner when the time came. Is there anybody you didn't use?"

Fraser looked offended. "Rebecca forced me to do this! You should arrest her!"

"For what?"

"For killing Mark, for a start!"

"But she didn't, did she? That was *you*."

Fraser's mouth was still open, ready to refute it. He slowly closed it and leaned back in his seat. The absence of denial was enough for Garrick. There had been a question mark over just who had killed Mark Kline-Watson. Now he knew.

"You just told me he wanted more money."

Fraser sighed and ran a hand through his hair. "He called me to say Rebecca had been down that morning demanding to know what had happened to Oscar. She knew he was our laundry man, so..." he shrugged. "Mark had a hold over me. Oscar was missing, I'd turned in a big chunk of money. I think he'd put two-and-two together."

"So he had to go."

Fraser didn't meet Garrick's gaze. He gave a slight nod.

"Meanwhile, Rebecca was still going ahead with the plan to get Terri out. That's when she went to pick up the cash from Matthews as arranged and saw there was just thirty grand there. She really thought Oscar had run off with the lot."

The only vaguely innocent person in all this mess was Terri Cordy. She may have known Oscar was unscrupulous, but she had faith that his dishonesty didn't extend to looking after his only son. Poor Huw Crawford had been drawn into hideous acts to win back the woman he loved. Whereas Rebecca Ellis was Oscar's accomplice in the heist, without knowing the man she loved was dead.

Quite a picture, Garrick thought dryly.

THERE WAS a muted atmosphere in the Incident room when Garrick returned. Chib, Fanta, and Wilkes had been writing up their case notes, but without the boisterous DC Harry Lord making them emergency brews every few minutes, it didn't feel like a time to celebrate. Fanta was irked that the collection for Harry had raised a pitiful eight pounds.

That wasn't helped when Harry made an unexpected entrance in a wheelchair, pushed by his wife, Claire. One leg was raised straight out in plaster, his arm in a sling. The swelling on his forehead had gone down, leaving a small cut stitched together.

"Don't worry! Lord is here to crack the case wide open!"

"You're too late, as usual," said Chib with a smirk. "Where have you been?"

Garrick snatched the collection cup before Fanta could put it in Harry's lap.

"There you go, mate. We had a whip-round."

Harry's face dropped when he counted it. "Eight quid?"

"Imagine what you would've got if you'd broken both legs."

Everybody roared with laughter, cracking the gloom that had been hanging over them. They debriefed him on the case, and Garrick even offered to make everybody a round of drinks to celebrate.

LATER, Superintendent Margery Drury took Garrick aside in her office to congratulate him. He filled in the details, and she listened without interruption. Garrick suggested they give Molly Meyer's the inside scoop. Thanks to her viral video, she had landed a job as an on-camera reporter for the BBC. She was a woman going places, and the Force could do with an ally in the media. Drury agreed.

Garrick was still stuffing himself with painkillers and was wondering if they were doing something to his senses, because despite the success, Drury looked pensive. Eventually, he found out why.

"We had an odd result from forensics. DC Liu picked it up and wasn't sure where it fitted in the evidence."

Garrick nodded, unsure where this was leading. "Okay."

"It was something you put in. An envelope."

Garrick winced. He'd forgotten about that.

"Is there something you want to tell me?"

He didn't. He had no intention of letting her know he thought he had heard his sister's voice, or that he was worried a possible brain tumour was making him hallucinate. Yet now he felt cornered.

"It arrived in the mail. The American postmark seemed odd. The fact it was empty was just weird."

Drury didn't blink as she studied him. "And that made you have it checked by a professional police forensics team?"

"I'm sorry, ma'am. I shouldn't have abused our resources. I didn't really think about it because of the case, and–"

Drury held up her hand to stop him.

"The misuse of police resources for personal reasons is one thing, David. Let's put that to one side for now. What did you expect they would find?"

Garrick scratched his head. The co-codamol was picking the wrong time to wear off.

"I honestly wasn't thinking straight. Maybe, where it had been posted from? I don't know anybody over there, except at Flora PD, and why would they send me it? Then I wondered if somebody here was trying to dick me around."

"Why would anybody want to do that?"

"You know how coppers are. Cruel tricks are our thing."

"It's sad that you think that."

Garrick said nothing in case he incriminated himself.

"The postmark was from New York. City, not State."

"Not Flora, then." Flora was a small town in Illinois, eight-hundred miles from New York.

"The thing is our labs are very thorough, and you didn't specify what you wanted them to focus on..."

Garrick felt a chill. "What was in the envelope?"

"Nothing."

"Okay."

"But it was sealed..." Drury hesitated as she worked out how to phrase it. "It was one of those old gum seals that you lick closed. There was DNA residue on that. It matches your sister's."

The sound of rain on the window grew louder. Garrick hadn't been aware of it. It felt as if it had poured down every day for weeks. If it wasn't for the wet weather, he mused, perhaps he would have been chopped into chum by the biplane's propellor. His mind was knitting random moments and marvelling how they could be brought together in a seemingly endless chain of cause and effect that could take a life or save one.

"Well?" Drury had been speaking, but he had zoned out. He didn't really care what she was saying.

"Sorry, what?"

"I said I had to notify the investigators in Flora PD. They want you to call them as soon as you can." Garrick slowly nodded. "There was something forensics pointed out. It wasn't saliva. A wet lip could have done it."

Garrick knew what she was hinting at. Saliva is only produced when alive. He nodded in understanding.

Drury looked increasingly worried. "This is unusual. Obviously. There is no escaping that you've been targeted to receive something calculated to worry you. Emelie still hasn't been found. Which means not only did they have access to her body, but this was also planned months ago."

The implications of her words jerked Garrick upright. "Why would somebody...?" He trailed off. That was an age-old question that human behaviour constantly invoked.

"David. If this was planned so long ago, then somebody in American must have a grudge against you. I need you to think about who."

"I don't know anybody over there. If that's the case, then maybe some villain I banged-up years ago."

"Somebody who could have targeted your sister."

Garrick's blood ran cold. That threw his entire perception about her murder on its head.

"Are you trying to suggest that she was killed to get at me?"

Drury anxiously tapped a finger on the desk. "No, David. I am telling you that is what Flora PD is now suggesting. They're worried that the letter was a warning."

"A warning about what?"

"That you're next."

30

J ust that a case had been solved, a suspect arrested, and a confession given didn't mean the work was over. Tying everything up, preparing evidence for the court case, getting extra witness statements, it was all a long and tedious process.

Rebecca Ellis had been arrested for accessory to armed robbery at Gatwick Airport as she attempted to board an Easyjet flight to Lisbon. She had checked in the two holdalls filled with Terri's possessions and the thirty thousand pounds Fraser had left behind.

Terri Cordy was cautioned and told not to leave the country. Drury had instructed Garrick to go home but fearing isolation he stayed late and brought reporter Molly Meyers in to brief her on events. She grew excited with the possibilities of a special report. The Hoy incident had captured imaginations around the world. This exclusive would be seen everywhere.

Garrick felt a tremor of satisfaction that he'd helped her

career. As she chatted with the team, he noticed the glower Fanta treated the pretty freckled redhead to as Sean Wilkes flirted and played up his own involvement. He decided that wasn't his problem and excused himself to go home. The last thing he wanted today was to be interviewed on camera. But he couldn't even escape that.

TWO DAYS PASSED. The weekend loomed, and Garrick had made several calls to Wendy in which he apologised for forgetting to call her during the lunch hour, as he'd said he would at the start of the week. Not even talking to her after the Pizza Hut moment was unforgivable.

As ever, Wendy understood and went on to tell him how good-looking he was on the Newsnight extended report about the 'Hoy Murders' as they were now known. He had refused twice, but Molly had been very persuasive. He put on a suit jacket, a white shirt with the top two buttons unfastened, but had forgotten to shave. Wendy insisted he looked rugged, and she was now the envy of her colleagues in the school. Garrick still ached everywhere, so the thought of going for a weekend cross-country ramble with her sounded like torture. Instead, he suggested they take an easy walk along a beach on the Isle of Sheppey, one of his favourite fossil hunting sites, although he kept quiet about that. The weather was supposed to be mild, and Garrick found himself excited by the prospect. He vowed he would leave his phone at home too.

FRIDAY CAME, and the promise for clearer weather for tomorrow's date didn't look as if it would be fulfilled. A whole day behind his desk, writing up notes and double-checking evidence, had been a welcome, if mundane, distraction. For the last few days, he'd been migraine free and was wondering if the stress of the job was the trigger, rather than the intruder in his skull. He was also low on his prescribed painkillers. He'd been hitting them hard to keep the other aches and pains at bay.

Rather too hard.

With his head bowed against the rain, he strode out of Sainsbury's with his weekend supply of food in his worn jute bag-for-life. He darkly mused over whose life the phrase was referring to – the bag's or the owner's? His was so threadbare that it was ripe for euthanasia.

"David!"

Garrick did a double take as DCI Kane climbed from a car parked a few yards away. A black Hyundai i40. What the hell was going on?

"What are you doing here?"

Kane smiled thinly. "Looking for you."

There was no doubt in Garrick's mind that Kane had followed him. He thought back to the black Hyundai tailing him and Chib from Rebecca Ellis's Airbnb, and the one parked at the Chilston Park Hotel. Both times he had assumed it was Huw Crawford's vehicle. But maybe not. At least, not one of them...

"Small world," said Garrick.

"You're easily recognisable now that you're on the telly so often. Congratulations, by the way."

Garrick didn't respond. He glanced up at the night sky. "If you want to talk, let's do it some place dry."

"Okay."

"And on Monday. After you book an appointment."

Kane's pleasant smile vanished. "I'm not sure what's with the hostility. To be honest, I didn't want to waltz into the office to talk to you. I'm doing this as a courtesy." His tone had become icy. "I thought you should know about Eric Wilson."

Garrick cocked his head. Wilson, his old DS. They had been together on a case when he'd heard about his sister's murder. Since then, Wilson had been seconded up north. Garrick had emailed him, but he hadn't replied, and recent events had put him out of mind.

"Is he okay?"

"He's dead."

The words were like a punch to the gut. Eric Wilson was young, spirited, always fun, and with a fiancée and a bright career ahead.

"H-how? When?"

Kane studied him for a moment. "In the line of duty. I can't tell you more. I thought you should know now. I hear you got on well together. He had nothing but nice things to say about you."

Garrick's mouth ran dry. He had no words.

"Sorry." DCI Kane returned to his car.

Just before he could close the door, Garrick found his voice again. "How did you find out? I thought he was in Staffordshire and you're investigating John Howard?"

"You know how it is," Kane said obliquely, then slammed his door shut and reversed from the parking space.

Numb, Garrick watched him go. Shivering from the rain, he trotted across the car park to his Land Rover. His hands were shaking as he searched his pockets for the keys. He pulled out his phone first, then his wallet, and then finally his fob. As he unlocked the door, the phone vibrated with an email. It was from Dr Rajasekar. The results of his MRI were in and she needed to discuss them.

Garrick's finger hovered over the reply button.

Then he deleted the email.

It could wait.

Perhaps there were some things that shouldn't be known.

ALSO BY M.G. COLE

info@mgcole.com

or say hello on Twitter: @mgcolebooks

SLAUGHTER OF INNOCENTS

DCI Garrick 1

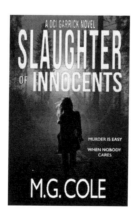

.

.

.

THE DEAD WILL TALK

DCI Garrick 3

MAY 2021

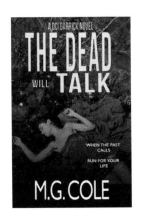